FESTIVAL OF THE VINE

A MAC AND MILLIE MYSTERY

JB MICHAELS

HARRISON AND JAMES PUBLISHING

TO MY WIFE, WHO MADE THIS ALL
POSSIBLE. YOUR LOVE IS ALL I NEED.

CHAPTER ONE

Friday night lights burn bright. The wind, a cool, crisp, early autumn force of nature, blows though the football field and onto the stands. The crowd cheers, jeers, and causes quite the ruckus at the game, perhaps, the biggest rivalry in the Fox River Valley: the Geneva Vikings verses the Batavia Bulldogs—and Geneva's homecoming game, nonetheless. A bold choice for the Geneva coaching staff to set the homecoming game against their biggest rivals. Usually, homecoming games were set against weak opponents the Vikings could bludgeon with their mighty maces. Not this year. No. The blue and white colors of Geneva High School fly high this fall.

The coaching staff thought they had a superior team. They could finally turn the tide of a decade-long losing streak against the Bulldogs. Oh, those nasty yellow and reddish-brown jerseys. Sorry: crimson and gold. That ugly English bulldog logo. Fitting for the Vikings to squash an English mascot, much like they terrorized merry old England long, long ago on their boats—so shallow on the draught that no river or inlet could stop them from their ferocious displays and ravenous raids of towns, villages, and settlements.

Beware you rabies-ridden, drooling, nasty bull-dogs. Here come the Vikings.

"Mac, it doesn't look good for our Vikings." Hank shook his head.

"There is still time. We have five minutes left! That's enough for maybe a possession or two!" Mac looked to the scoreboard. He gnashed his teeth in worry. The visiting Bulldogs were up by ten points. They'd just booted a field goal with a kid who looked like he could just kick for the Chicago Bears. The leg on that kid! He booted a fifty-five yarder!

"Well, at least they made it interesting for three quarters." Hank put his hands up, clearly already accepting defeat.

"Hank, again, there is still time."

Batavia kicked the ball off to the Vikings. The Geneva kickoff returner fielded the ball cleanly. He ran a few yards to the middle of his blockers tight formation in front of him. The kid, number 23, followed his blocks then, like Devin Hester, he found a seam and turned on the jets. The kickoff returner ran to the Batavia forty.

The thirty.

The twenty.

The Batavia kicker's long arms nearly clipped the returner's foot, but he kept running.

Mac yelled, "Go! Go! Go! Go!"

Hank stood up from the steel bleacher and smiled.

"TOUCHDOWN! VIKINGS!" Mac yelled. Over the loudspeaker, the announcer yelled the same phrase with similar gusto. The cheerleaders raised their pompoms and chanted Valhalla. Well, maybe not Valhalla, but Mac liked to think so.

"Down four. With just over four minutes to go. We can do this!" Hank yelled, suddenly bouncing out from his once forlorn outlook.

"Yes, we can Hank. Yes. We. Can!" Mac grabbed Hank's shoulders.

"Hahaha! And the extra point is good. Down three!"

"We just need the defense to hold. The line

looks tired. Batavia's running back doesn't seem to get tired. Let's hope they don't bleed the clock!"

"MOM! Go easy on the wine. How many glasses is that for you?" Millie's eyes were wide.

The special preview wine-tasting night for Geneva's famous Festival of the Vine commenced. Mac and Becca attended with tickets given to Millie by her boss, Gerald, at Salem Bank.

"Millie, please, you know I don't drink that often." Becca laughed.

"Mom, you also shouldn't shotgun wine. Drink it slowly, savor it."

"Don't tell me what to do, Millie. We should get some tacos soonish, I think. Don't you think?"

Millie couldn't even respond. She just forced a smile. Becca was handily buzzed, if not completely drunk, at this point in the evening. They stood on Third Street in front of the Geneva courthouse and Millie wondered if they had any holding cells that she could just fling her mother into for the rest of the night.

It was 8:30. The event started at 8. Becca was already feeling good in that short amount of time. People milled about the event and Becca's sisters,

Millie's aunts, joined their group. They were both blonde. All of them were blonde, Millie just enhanced her hair with silver tones. Her hair looked gray, if anything.

Mary and Sherry laughed at their older sister.

"You never could handle drinking alcohol, Beck. You are embarrassing your daughter!" Sherry said.

"I don't know, you guys. She seems perfectly fine to me." Mary took a big swig of her wine. "Like she can handle it and I don't know if that is good or bad."

Becca beamed. "See! I am fine. Thank you, Mary. Seriously, though, tacos?"

CHAPTER TWO

The turnover happened on the fifty yard line. A sign from Valhalla that the Geneva Vikings actually had a legitimate chance to win the game or, at least, tie. The two-minute mark ticked on the game clock.

"I can't believe this!" Mac put his hands on the top of his head.

"They have one timeout. They don't need to force it. Plenty of time." Hank's years of coaching sports kicked in. He coached Angela and Millie for many years while they were growing up. He loved sports. At 272 Witchhazel Circle, there's always a sports game on the television. Just don't ask him to drive into Chicago for a live game. *Too much of a hassle.* He hated traffic.

A high school football game five minutes from home, however, proved ideal.

"Here we go—the time has come!"

The white and blue jerseys of the Geneva Viking offensive football team took the field. The noise from the stands grew louder and louder. Excitement filled the air. A win against their fiercest opponents was within reach and with just under two minutes left.

The quarterback dropped back to pass. He looked left, then right, then let the pigskin fly. The ball seemed to hang in the air, of course, as if in slow motion, but sailed out of bounds.

A minute and fifty seconds left on the clock.

Hank and Mac stared at the field. Superstition reared its neurotic head. Mac started rubbing his chin incessantly. Hank crossed his arms across his chest and tapped his arm with his left hand.

Second down.

Running play.

Halfback toss. Gain of fifteen yards.

The clock was still running with just a buck thirty left. Geneva Coach Rigby used both hands to make a T for timeout.

The ball was on the thirty-five yard line.

"They aren't going to kick a field goal now, are they?" Mac asked.

"No. No. Too much time left." Hank kept tapping that arm.

The offense ran back out onto the field.

The Batavia Bulldogs crowded the line of scrimmage.

"They are bringing pressure." Mac squeezed his chin.

The ball snapped.

It was an all out blitz. The Geneva quarterback got slammed down hard by a linebacker, number fifty-one, in maroon and yellow.

The clock was running now, ticking down to a minute.

Mac bit his knuckle. "Ah, they lost almost ten yards!"

Third down and forever. The center snapped the ball to the quarterback and the QB kept the ball. He ran behind the halfback for a sweep and the far side-line opened up—he ran and ran to the fifteen yard line before being pushed out of bounds.

"First down and we save some clock!" Hank yelled.

The clock stopped with thirty-five seconds left.

Coach Rigby quickly gave the quarterback the play, which probably was "give the ball to Thirty-Four," the stud running back on the Viking offensive squad. It was risky and would drain the clock more than an incomplete pass or quick pass for a first, but the best player needed to be the rock in this situation.

Ball snapped, with a quick toss to Thirty-Four on the same sideline that opened up before. This time... not so much. The Bulldogs flowed to that side of the field and stopped the Viking running back after only a couple yards.

The clock ticked down to twenty-five seconds and counting.

"They need to spike the ball. Clock it." Mac patted Hanks' back then went back to biting his knuckle.

The Geneva QB drove the ball directly into the ground and stopped the clock at nineteen ticks. Rigby ran to the sideline and yelled the play.

The crowd in the stands were loud, with Batavia's fans causing much of the ruckus. Mac's ears started to hurt a bit. The Vikings fans weren't as loud, as the suspense proved too great to vocalize. The Vikings had, maybe, two plays left to try and get into the end zone.

CHAPTER THREE

Ball on the thirteen yard line.

Second down.

Ball snapped.

It's a play action fake to Thirty-Four and the QB rolled out to the near sideline. He fired a pass to the tight end on the sideline near the five yard line: he caught it and then ran out of bounds.

Third down and two yards to go for the first down.

Only eight seconds on the clock.

Ball snapped. QB faked a run and then lateralled to number Thirty-Four, the running back, who made a hell of a cut off tackle opposite the flow of the Batavia defense that bit on the quarterback's direction and momentum.

Number Thirty-Four leaped into the end zone!

"Touchdoooooooown!" Mac yelled and jumped up and down, ignoring the pain in his bad leg. He even dropped his cane.

The Viking crowd erupted and the sideline poured into the end zone. Soon enough, the cheerleaders joined the fray along with first few rows of fans from the stands. Energetic cries of joy and berserker energy from the mighty warrior tradition of Scandinavian culture struck the football arena like lightning followed by a resounding thunderbolt from Thor's hammer.

Pure joy. Catharsis. The bulldog off the Viking's back.

"We did it!" Hank slapped Mac a five.

The celebration poured out onto the field and Hank and Mac were one of the few left in the stands. It was the perfect time for Mac to ask Hank what he should have asked in the summer at Swedish Days, but extenuating circumstances prevented the question and subsequent conversation.

With Hank riding the high of victory, perhaps now would be best.

"Hey Hank, what a game!" He sucked in a sharp breath. "Hank, can I ask you something?"

"Sure Mac, what is it?" Hank took a seat on the silver bleacher bench.

Mac did the same and then picked up his cane and held it tight—thanks to both adrenaline and nerves.

"Well, I wanted to ask you for your daughter's hand in marriage. May I marry your daughter?" Mac just blurted it out. He felt immediate, short-lived relief and then the nerves struck back. His stomach twisted.

"Angela is already married." Hank smiled.

"Ha! I meant Millie, of course."

"The answer is no."

Mac's eyes went wide. "Are you..."

"Hahaha! Of course, you can marry her. We would love to have you as part of the family!" Hank put his hand out for Mac to shake.

Mac obliged and shook his hand. "Thank you, sir. She really is an incredible woman and a great partner. Thank you so much. I promise to take great care of her."

"You better! I have my hands full already with Becca."

Mac laughed.

The crowd started to disperse and leave the football field. The team went back into the locker room to wrap things up and start their celebrations. A few people had stayed back and milled about, when a girl near the goal post started to scream.

Not just any scream, but very loud and blood curdling. "Help!"

CHAPTER FOUR

Mac couldn't even relish the moment he just shared with Hank, his hopefully future father-in-law as long as Millie said yes. He went into full cop-mode and used his cane to hasten his descent of the bleacher's steep steps. He looked to the goal post and the girl who cried out for help: she stood next to a person laying on the ground.

Hopefully, the person was just unconscious and not, of course, deceased. Mac usually seemed to run into the dead since living in the quaint and apparently, deadly, town of Geneva.

"Hey Mac, want me to call an ambulance?" Hank yelled from higher up in the stands.

"Yes, go ahead. Wait, looks like an officer is

already over there. You can head out if you want. I will meet you back at 272."

"Okay, I will see you later." Hank waved. "Good luck!"

Mac made his way down to the cushy track that separated the sideline from the stands and walked to the goalpost.

"He's not breathing." The Geneva officer said to Mac.

"Have you tried CPR at all?"

"I did, but blood kept pouring from his chest."

Mac examined the young man. Early 20s. He wore a Geneva High School blue fleece sweater now soaked with blood from his chest wound. He also had a silly inaccurate Viking helmet on, the kind with the big horns.

He was clearly dead.

Mac bent down and examined his chest. A small sliver of a tear in his sweater showed the wound: a stab wound right to the heart. He searched the surrounding area for the knife or stabbing weapon that most likely caused the bleeding and subsequent death.

Five people, students and one adult, still crowded the dead body and Mac. If there was evidence in the end zone, they might contaminate it.

"If everyone can just take a step back, maybe to the five yard line, that would help." He waved his hands at the group, motioning them backwards. "Officer, can you make sure they step back so we can set up a perimeter here? Don't let anyone leave."

"Yes, Officer O'Malley, okay folks you heard him. Let's just line up on the five yard line. Give us some space." The uniformed police officer put his hands in front of him and walked the crowd out of the end zone and back to the five.

"Mac! What we got?" The silver-haired sibling and GPD Detective Vince ran to the scene of the crime from behind the stands.

"Looks like we got a stabbing victim, but I can't find the weapon just yet. Help me find it." Mac said, circling the victim with his head down.

"Well this is a mess and right after we win the ballgame, too. Damnit." Vince reached the crime scene. He kept shaking his head in frustration.

"I don't see the weapon anywhere." Mac shook his head. The bright Friday night lights showed nothing but green grass.

"You check underneath him?" Vince knelt down and pushed the young man's body to its side.

"No, not yet. I was going to let you do the honors."

"Gee thanks. Here it is: a knife. Serrated." Vince just observed and didn't touch it quite yet. "Nasty thing, too. Sharp."

"Direct hit to his heart and bled out fast." Mac fell silent for a moment and then said, "I have seen a knife and a wound like this before."

CHAPTER FIVE

Mac felt a pit grow in his stomach. A large one. It was penetrating, painful and a cause of much anguish. He saw a young man with a similar wound ten years ago. Kid was barely an adult. His license said he'd just turned eighteen. The kid called the police and Mac and his partner didn't make it in time. Kid got caught up in the wrong crowd. Made dumb mistakes.

Usually these situations were taken care of with a small caliber handgun. The viciousness of the kill is what bothered Mac: a dagger with no other reason for existence except for the killing blow. The likelihood Mac would run into a comparable stabbing weapon in the same spot. Right in the heart.

"Mac, you okay?" Vince looked up from his notebook.

"Yeah, it's fine." Mac nodded his head. "We have an ID on this guy yet?"

The uniform came back over from the five yard line. "Coach Gainor, assistant coach for the Vikes."

"If he was a coach, why was he was wearing a mascot helmet?" Vince asked.

"Maybe a celebratory hat? Not totally out of the realm of possibility, Vince, they did just get a big win. Wound looks fresh. Someone in the crowd did it on the sly and just walked away." Mac stitched together his theory out loud. Sometimes that helped.

"Possibly. Let's leave it to the medical examiner. Medics are on the way. I will take care of the kids here, talk to them and find out what they saw. You can head home, Mac. You really don't have to do this anymore—for the love of God." Vince laughed.

"You are right, I really should just get home. I am tired. Anyway, big day tomorrow for Millie and I... I'm going to ask her to marry me." Mac smiled.

"I can't believe you are telling me this in front of stabbing victim. What the hell is wrong with you? This job has literally deranged your mind. Come here, you idiot!" Vince put his arms out to give his brother a hug.

Mac embraced his brother. It made him feel better in the moment. Vince gave great hugs: big bear hugs. Mac wasn't exactly small, but Vince was older and bigger. Mac felt better in his brother's embrace.

The hug was his only respite from the disparate feeling he had. That sinking feeling. Something felt wrong. Very wrong.

But he took his brother's advice. "Okay, Vince, you are right. Love you. I will call you no matter what she says."

"She'll probably say no." Vince pulled back from the hug and put his hands on Mac's shoulders.

"Ha! Very funny! Second time I heard that tonight. Ah, whatever. Good luck getting to the bottom of this one." Mac walked away and looked up to the bright Friday night lights, leaned heavily on his cane, and headed back to the parking lot.

He looked down at the grass and breathed in the chilly early autumn evening air. Mac forced himself to accept his happiness. *It is okay to stop solving crimes. It is okay to accept a new life as an author and crime novelist.* Tomorrow, he would finally propose to the love of his life. Then, they'd have a few glasses of wine and enjoy the Festival of the Vine.

Mac reached for the door handle of his Cinderella blue sedan. He stopped his hand inches from grasping the handle, instead digging into his coat pocket and pulling out his phone. Time to call Millie. He wanted to see how she was, but also figure out what to do next. Maybe she could help him shake the funk he found himself in after seeing the knife and yet another dead body.

"Hello, thank God you called. Help me. Mom is super drunk." Millie's gentle and calm tone did much to help Mac in the moment.

"Oh, no way. What is Becca like totally hammered?"

"Hungry for greasy food, for one thing. What's up? You and Dad headed home?"

"Your Dad is probably already back at 272. I stayed behind because, of course, something bad happened. I swear, I feel like I can't go out to any major event in the Fox River Valley without some sort of tragedy happening!"

"Oh no. What happened?" Millie's voice dropped an octave. "Not another murder?"

"Yes, unfortunately, an assistant coach for Geneva, stabbed in the heart. Young guy, early 20s."

"Oh jeez, Mom...Mom stop. I don't want to hear about you and Dad in that particular situation. Sorry, Mom is attempting to overshare with her DAUGH-TER! I'm sorry, Mac, did Vince make it there?"

Mac laughed then composed himself. "Yes, he is there and taking care of it. I just can't seem to shake this feeling I got after I saw the knife. It brought me back to a rough case with a kid, that's all. Ugh."

"Mac, we know how things go when you get one of those feelings. Just stay there and help Vince. I will check in with you later. You don't want to be around the situation I'm in either. I'm in a drive thru with Mom...so yeah, there's that. Love you and see you tomorrow."

"Okay, sounds good. Thanks Millie. Maybe you are right: maybe I could help Vince a bit more. Love you too and yes: tomorrow, come hell or high water, will be great. Festival of the Vine will be divine!" Mac assured. He wasn't sure who he intended his words to comfort more, him or Millie. He needed convincing that he wasn't cursed in some way.

"It will be. Okay, talk to you later." Millie ended the call.

Mac put his phone back in his pocket and then looked back to the bright lights. The ambulance pulled in and they were now removing the body from the field. Uniforms and Vince and Jackson had set up the crime scene and were examining the site.

No matter how dire the circumstance. No matter how grim his feelings were. Mac's heart still pumped with excitement when another mystery needed solving. He couldn't help himself. The thrill of the hunt, the stimulation, and, like Millie said, those feelings: instincts that can't be manufactured through training.

Mac wanted to question the coaching staff first. Maybe they would have some clue as to what happened when the medical examiner finalized the report.

CHAPTER SEVEN

Mac O'Malley walked into the locker room of the victorious Vikings. The players were rowdy and still celebrating. Mac knew that the celebration would end quickly and imminently. The air was heavy with rank body odor and he had to be careful not to slip from the sweat that dripped off the team members. Stinky teenage boys. Not Mac's idea of fun on a Friday night.

Still, he just had to make it to the wooden door with the head coach's name on it. Just...at the other end of the narrow, slick and stinky corridor of the locker room.

"Excuse me, gentlemen. Is your coach in his office?"

"Yep! He just finished up with us. He is. Head

on in! We won baby! Yeah!" An excited linemen hopped up and down and pumped his fists.

"Thanks. If you could just clear a path for me, that would be great." Mac smiled.

"Oh shit. Yeah. Hey, let the man through. He has to see da coach!"

The ten kids on the right side of the bench jumped to the left and cleared a path for Mac.

"Thank you! Great game tonight fellas! Keep it up!" Mac pumped his fist.

"Hell yeah!"

Lots of hooting and hollering later, Mac finally made it to the door. It was partially open. The smell of cheap aftershave emanated from the room behind the door. Mac frowned at the smell, then entered the small office.

Coach Rigby sat at his desk with his head down. The books and binders on his shelf were on the floor, his desk drawers pulled out and its contents emptied onto the floor. The news apparently reached him before the team found out.

"Hey Coach. I am Officer Mac O'Malley. I take it you heard the bad news?"

"Yes. Do we have to have this conversation now, Officer? I had all of ten minutes to savor my victory over Batavia and my assistant coach winds up dead on the field." Coach Rigby didn't lift his head.

"Honestly, Coach. If you would just cooperate, it would help us and give your assistant coach's family a shot at justice. We need to gather as much information on him as we can, as soon as we can. Make sense? How did you find out?"

"Tim, the equipment manager, just texted me. I heard the damn sirens and knew something was up. Ask away, Officer. Clearly you aren't leaving." Rigby finally lifted his head. He was overweight with a big mustache and a red face. Big guy. Tall and wide.

Mac took a deep breath. He felt the urge to whack the guy on his giant head with his cane, but restrained himself. He clenched his teeth and tightened his grip on his cane.

"Well, have you noticed anything different about your assistant coach lately?"

"Yes. He has been hanging out with too many of the young cheerleaders. He also was engaged to my daughter. So, yeah, there's that." Rigby had an aggressive tone, like he was a kettle ready to scream at the boiling point.

"Just for clarification. What exactly does 'hanging out' with young cheerleaders mean? Was he acting inappropriately with them or towards them? Is that what you mean?"

"No, nothing bad per se. But he has been very friendly towards one of them lately."

"You sure he didn't have any connection to this cheerleader? Like a cousin or something?" Mac pressed.

"No, I don't know anything like that. Her name is Lacey Gonzalez. Thing is, she isn't even a Geneva cheerleader. She's a Batavia kid. But I saw her and him a few times together around town. I have no idea why, and frankly, I didn't want to confront him. I got enough on my plate with coaching and teaching to even give a shit about what he does...or did, I should say."

"Did you tell your daughter about him and Lacey?"

"Again, no. I haven't said anything to anybody. Can you please leave me be? I have to talk to my team about this before they leave and it ruins their damn victory night."

"One more question. What is your daughter's name?"

"Misty. Now, it's all of a sudden too quiet in the locker room. I'm sure the news has reached the team. Thanks, Officer."

Mac nodded and walked out before Rigby. The few team members left in the locker room looked forlorn, heartbroken. The pit that earlier formed in Mac's gut grew deeper and wider as the night wore on.

CHAPTER EIGHT

Misty Rigby. She was the next person he needed to interview, but he had no idea how to contact her. And, these days, the yellow pages weren't exactly easy to come by.

Mac walked back out onto the field. The paramedics were loading the body into the ambulance. Vince stood at the scene, rubbing his neck. A perimeter of yellow police tape now hung from the goal post and to the sideview mirrors of a couple squad cars. His brother stared at the grass, deep in thought.

"Vincey. Misty Rigby—she here with Gainor tonight?" Mac ducked under the tape and walked to his brother.

Vince pulled out his small notepad. "No, I didn't

get a Misty Rigby on the people who discovered the body. Jackson, do a quick residential search for a Misty Rigby."

Jackson hopped back into his unmarked squad car to type into the computer on the front console.

"I thought you were gonna get home and get some damn rest, Mac." Vince reviewed the notes on his notepad. His expression was still perplexed.

"What's wrong?" Mac asked.

"A stab to the heart should pool more blood and the knife wasn't even that bloody. I mean, let's face it, the heart is the pumping organ. Kind of a big deal. Can't figure out why there's so little blood evidence."

"Well, that sounds like the medical examiner's forte. That is an interesting point. The blades of grass should be bloodier and his body didn't seem to have that much blood pouring from the wound. That isn't the only strange thing about Coach Gainor."

"What else?"

"I talked to the head coach, Rigby. Said Gainor was dating his daughter Misty and that he had been hanging around a young cheerleader from Batavia. A Lacey Gonzalez. The Coach seemed pissed and was gonna confront Gainor about it."

"Hmm, that's interesting...and you are going to interview Misty next? I see. Let me know how that goes. I will mop up here, ah, even though there really isn't much to mop up. Still, I will do my due diligence on my end and let you know if anything crazy comes up. Jackson, you got that address?!" Vince yelled.

"The new Schroeder Condominium complex. Third Street and the tracks." Jackson yelled from the car window.

"Okay, Vince, I will keep you updated. Got it. Thanks!" Mac nodded his head towards Jackson.

MAC PARKED in front of the new green siding and limestone decorated building on the end of the premiere drag of the Geneva downtown area, Third Street. Rigby seemed quite upset with Gainor, but would he kill his daughter's boyfriend on such a special night? The Batavia-Geneva rivalry game—and Homecoming as well? Nah. He may have been upset with Gainor for hanging out with Lacey, a young cheerleader, but probably not enough to escalate to murder. Maybe Misty could help clarify a few sticking points.

Mac enjoyed the crisp fall air, but it did make his bum leg hurt a bit more. Cold air seeped into his already aching bones and stuck there, as if trapped in the marrow. He leaned on the cane just a bit more than he normally did. What a crazy evening.

He reached for the door handle when something crashed on the sidewalk next to him. It hit the ground with a smack, plastic shrapnel pieces bouncing around and hitting his jacket. It looked like a video game console. He looked up and a white dress shirt floated down, followed by some jeans and khaki slacks. Flashes of medieval castle warfare ignited in Mac's imagination: bubbling hot oil poured from the ramparts.

What the hell was going on?

CHAPTER NINE

A domestic dispute most likely. An affair uncovered. A break-up made more hurtful since the once happy couple did cohabitate, given the amount and nature of the presumably male occupant's goods being tossed out a second story window at Mac.

"Excuse me! Could you please stop?" Mac put his free arm over his head to block the debris.

"What?" A distraught female voice called from the balcony above.

"Yes, yes. If you could please stop throwing stuff at me, I would appreciate it. Say, you wouldn't' t happen to know which unit Misty Rigby is in, do you?"

"I'm Misty. What do you want?" Misty put both hands on her railing and stared down at Mac, her hair a curly light brown mess. She was athletically built, strong, with mascara running down her cheeks.

"I am sorry Misty. I am Officer Mac O'Malley." Mac shuffled for his retired badge and showed it to her in the yellow ambient light of the dim street lamps.

"What happened?" Misty asked. She apparently didn't know what happened to Coach Gainor.

"May I come up or you can come down here? I just have a few questions to ask."

"Come on up. I will buzz you in." Misty disappeared from the balcony.

Mac walked to the doors and the buzzer droned for a second before he opened the door. The heated air of the condo building felt good. The crisp fall evening grew colder by the second, but the ache in his leg lessened in intensity with the warm air.

He made his way up the stairs to the second floor where Misty waited with the hall door open.

"What happened, Officer?" Misty's eyes were wide.

Mac dreaded situations like this. The bearer of bad news role didn't suit him or frankly, anyone in their right mind. Let's be real. The news of a loved one's death is just about the most unwelcome type of news. Absolutely horrendous.

"Why don't we get into your place and have a seat? I just think it would be best."

"Oh no, is it my Dad? His heart? He takes the Batavia game too seriously. Oh no!" Misty jumped to conclusions. Her neurosis in full gear and her imagination in overdrive wasn't surprising, given her emotional state upon Mac's arrival: tossing Gainor's clothes and video game systems out of windows.

Misty and Mac walked into the brand new condo. It had beautiful wood flooring and a shiplap accent wall in the dining room, to the right of the entrance. Misty and Mac sat at the table.

"Officer. Please. I have had a hell of a week." Misty pleaded, running her hands through her curly mop.

"Coach Gainor was found murdered on the field after the victory celebration." Mac just ripped off the proverbial bandage as fast as possible. He found, over the years, that was the best thing to do.

Misty fell silent. She stopped fiddling. Her face turned red. She took a deep breath, as if a storm of conflicting emotions toiled inside of her: anger, sadness, guilt...possibly even a primal satisfaction?

"Were you at the game this evening?"

"Hell no, I wasn't. I was with my friends at the Wine Cellar across the street. I just got back. Coach

Gainor just recently broke up with me. I loved that man very dearly, I wouldn't have—" Misty put her hands over her mouth and screamed in agony.

"Misty, I am really sorry. Can I ask you a few more questions?"

She moaned and mumbled.

Mac shook his head. "Maybe you shouldn't be alone right now. Can you call a friend over? I will wait here." Mac felt awful. Still, he couldn't let her have too long of a leash. She clearly had motive: a broken heart.

Misty planted her face in her crossed arms on the table. Her voice was muffled as she said, "Please come back later. Please."

"I will be in touch, Misty. Please don't skip town or anything. I still have a few questions to ask you." Mac stood up and walked out of the condo.

Time to head across the street before the wine bar closed. Misty was probably there the whole night, just like she said.

Right?

CHAPTER TEN

Misty Rigby needed some supervision. Mac realized the Rigby family suffered from anger management issues, as his second encounter with them turned out the way that it did.

"Vince, might want to get a squad to keep an eye on the Schroeder apartments at the end of Third Street, just before the tracks."

"Why? What happened?"

"Mistry Rigby. She is distraught and may have had motive to off her ex-boyfriend of just a few days: Coach Gainor." Mac rubbed his leg as he shuffled across the street to the Wine Cellar.

"So, they just broke up and now the guy winds up dead. Jeez, that may be enough to bring her in, Mac! You just left?" Vince asked.

"Well, yes, but she says she was at the Geneva Wine Cellar during and after the game. I am headed there to check her alibi. Like I said, I don't think she is a flight risk, but have someone monitor the area for her. Just in case."

"Okay, fine. I'll send a squad over there. Let me know what else you find. If she's anything like her father, she's a piece of work. That guy is real testy and not particularly sad at all. I guess it *has* been a hell of a night for him. The game went really well and then one of his coaches gets offed on his field of victory. Okay, everything is pretty boring over here. We're mopping up and none of the football players noticed anything strange with Gainor, so we are all good there. Talk later; I'll call you if I hear anything from the examiner. Out." Vince ended the call.

Mac walked across the street and north a little ways to another limestone construction. The Geneva Wine Cellar, home to a nice wine bar and tasting area for many a bachelorette party and evening event. They, of course, had the place decked out. The specials were displayed everywhere, with intricately worded ingredients that encouraged drinkers to consume with aplomb and without prejudice. After all, it was Festival of the Vine weekend.

There were about four people left inside the bar

area. The middle-aged brunette female behind the counter had already cleaned the bar and looked as if she was readying the cellar for close. "Can I help you, sir? We are closing in about ten minutes, but I can still get you a glass."

"No, thank you. I was just wondering if a curly-haired brunette named Misty was in here from about 7 to 10pm or so tonight?"

"We had a really busy night and are prepping for an even busier weekend. We had many people in here. I am sorry, I don't know. Who are you anyway? You look familiar."

"Oh right, I'm sorry. Detective Mac O'Malley. I am new in town...just under a year I suppose still constitutes as new." Mac again flashed his retired badge. He covered the retired lettering underneath the star.

"Oh, that's right! That is right. The hero of the Chicago Marathon well, almost, bombing. Here, I think I have a merlot still open that some customers didn't drink. Want any? I'm Annie, by the way. I own the Cellar along with my husband." Annie poured a glass of red wine into a stemless glass.

"I really shouldn't, but if you have it, sure, why not! Thanks so much. So, you don't remember anyone named Misty in here tonight?" Mac picked up the glass and gave the wine a sip. He didn't drink much, but maybe this would help clear his head a bit and maybe take a slight edge off his aching leg.

"I can check the receipts. Give me a couple minutes." Annie opened a drawer and filed through some receipts.

Mac took another sip. Really more of a gulp. He didn't have the patience to not suck down alcoholic beverages, which is why he didn't imbibe with any consistent frequency. Alcoholism ran in the O'Malley clan.

"Ah! Here we go. Misty Rigby signed her receipt at about 10:03pm. She in trouble? What happened?" Annie showed Mac a very neatly signed receipt in cursive form.

"Her ex-boyfriend was murdered today at the football field. Just wanted to cover all our bases. She said she was here and her alibi checks out." Mac took another swig and finished the glass of wine.

"Glad I could help. That is just awful. Another murder! And at the football field with all those kids around!" Annie put her hand on her chest.

"The GPD will get to the bottom of it. No need to worry. You will notice some more squads rolling by tonight. Don't be alarmed, as they are here for your protection. Thanks again for the wine!" Mac smiled.

Time to get to Batavia and to the Gonzalez household. Misty Rigby was cleared thus far. Still, she seemed quite upset with Gainor and the situation. She could have had him murdered. If she could afford a nice apartment on Third Street, then money probably wasn't an issue. Sitting at the Wine Cellar during the game was a perfect alibi. Mac only noticed one bottle on the bill of sale. So, either she paid for the bottle for two people, or her other friends, or she and her friends asked for separate checks.

Misty's alibi checked out, but Mac didn't feel her innocence. Something felt strange and it wasn't the wine talking.

Mac called the GPD to look up info on a Lacey Gonzalez enrolled in Batavia High School. They gave an address in a residential area off Fabyan Parkway. Mac pulled into a neighborhood that was surrounded by trees and very lush greenery, the houses basically in the forest. There was lots of great shade, but with the absence of light posts it was difficult to see the addresses on the somewhat older homes. There weren't even sidewalks in this area. Just grass, homes, and rather narrow roadways.

The Gonzalez household was a nice ranch with many flowers on the porch and perfectly coiffed bushes. The flowers still had petals clinging to the stem as the chill of autumn bit the night air. The home sat on a road that backed up to the forest on two sides of the house. The end of the road was marked by the forest as well as the rear of the property.

"Looks like the end of the road here." Mac said to himself as he closed the door to his blue sedan.

He walked down a cracked sidewalk to the front porch. The lights weren't on. The only light emanated from the moon's feint glow. The cast iron sign was nailed to the white siding of the house: Number 456.

Mac checked his phone for the time. It was nearing 11 o'clock. Someone in the Gonzalez house had to be up, especially the teenaged Lacey. He rang the doorbell. A murder investigator didn't worry himself with the niceties of civilian life. He had a job to do, no matter the time of day.

A porch light sparked on to the left of Mac's head.

"Yes, hello. May I help you?" A man with a decent sized beer belly and a white t-shirt answered the door. He didn't look as if he'd been woken from sleep. He stood behind the screen door alert and wide awake.

"Mr. Gonzalez?" Mac asked with a smile on his face. The sound of a late night comedy talk show played in the background.

"Yes. What is it?"

"I am Officer Mac O'Malley. I was wondering if I could speak with Lacey. I just want to ask her a few questions about the football game she was at tonight."

"Sorry Officer, Lacey is in bed. I don't want to disturb her. Can't this wait until morning?"

"I am afraid that it would be best if you could just wake her up. It won't take long, I promise."

"She in trouble? Maybe I can help answer your questions. I know that she was at the game tonight." Mr. Gonzalez breathed deeply. He clearly didn't really want to help.

"If I can just talk to her, I can easily clear things up. It's just that one of the Geneva coaches passed away tonig—."

Mr. Gonzalez slammed the door on his face.

It was going to be a long night. Possibly a very long night. Mac just bit his bottom lip and shook his head.

He turned around. His phone vibrated in his front pocket.

"Vincey, what's happening, brother?" Mac walked on the cracked sidewalk back to his car.

"Got a quick update from the medical examiner. Get this. The cause of death was not from the stab wound." Vince's voice sounded deep and rather grim.

"What? We found a knife wound and a knife under his body."

"Yes, we did. But remember, there was not that much blood in the grass. Turns out the kid suffered massive internal bleeding in his chest. Like one of his ventricles burst before the knife even went into his chest," Vince said.

Mac threw his cane on the passenger seat and started his car.

"So, he had a heart condition? Any prints on the knife?"

"Yes, they belong to the disgruntled ex Misty Rigby. She works for Argonne National Labs. She was in the database. I have the squad already bringing her in. Want to stop by for some interrogation fun?"

"If he didn't die from the knife wound, we could still get her for attempted murder I suppose. Jeez, I thought this would be a longer night but man, things are now looking easy peezy. Yes, I'll head to the station now. I went to ask that Lacey Gonzalez kid some questions, but the dad shut the door in my face. Said to come back tomorrow morning."

"Yeah, we can worry about that tomorrow. We

have a weapon and prints and a motive. We may not have to ask Lacey anything."

"Misty's alibi checked out though. There is a bill of sale with a time stamp and everything for the Geneva Wine Cellar."

"Come on, Mac. Anyone can use anyone's card at any time. Let's just do our job and ask her the questions." Vince laughed, probably in the hope that he'd get to go home soon and just shut this newly opened case.

"You're right. Okay, see you soon." Mac pulled away from the Gonzalez's, hoping he wouldn't have to return.

CHAPTER TWELVE

Misty Rigby sat in the small interrogation room. She looked distraught. Pissed. Not at all ready to cooperate. The fluorescent bulbs over her head showed her frizzy, curly hair and overall tired look, complete with bags under her eyes and red marks on her cheeks. The shock of being brought in had given way to complete rage. Mac thought she might even pounce on him and Vince.

"I talked to you earlier. Why didn't you just ask me to come in? Why all the drama of being taken out of my condo?" Misty shot a scary, wide-eyed look at Mac.

"I didn't think I needed to bring you in." Mac stood in the corner and leaned on his cane.

Vince took a seat right in front of her. "Misty. I

really don't think you are in a position of strength here. Officer O'Malley's judgement need not be criticized by someone with motive to murder their ex on the football field after a great Geneva victory."

Vince didn't pull any punches.

"I didn't kill Tim. That is ridiculous! I told you I was at the Wine Cellar during and after the game. Yes, he dumped me a few days ago, but I didn't kill him!" Misty's voice was filled with bitterness and spite.

"We have a knife with your prints on it. A steak knife. Sharp. Pointed and big enough to rupture someone's heart. Your prints were on it. Explain why Tim Gainor had a knife sticking out of his chest." Vince pressed.

"A steak knife? He took that from my house. He slept over most nights. That's an easy explanation, you morons." Misty didn't mince words. She also had severe issues with authority.

"He took the knife from your house?"

"Yes, he would take utensils out of the house all the time and use them to make his lunch at work. That's not uncommon. I want my knife back."

"You want the knife that was stuck in the chest of your dead ex-boyfriend?" Mac chimed in.

"Yes, why not? It was mine." She almost stood up to yell at Mac.

"You didn't answer the question. Explain how Tim had *your* knife from *your* kitchen collection in his chest."

"I don't know how that happened. I wasn't there. I was at the Wine Cellar drinking wine trying to forget that asshole. Why for the love of God would I murder him? I loved him! I still love him!" Misty put her head in her hands. She sniffled.

"Vince, can I see you out in the hallway?" Mac pointed his cane to the door.

Vince stood up and walked out. Mac followed and shut the door. Misty's sobs were audible from behind the closed door.

"She's telling the truth. This is bizarre. The knife—did it have any other prints on it or smudges like a glove handled it at any point?"

"No, it only had their prints on it. The handle wasn't textured and we were able to actually pull the prints from it. There were no glove smudges. They both handled the knife, most likely only the two of them." Vince rubbed the stubble on his chin.

"So, if she didn't plunge the knife into his chest, Coach Gainor must have plunged it into his chest himself? But why? Is that really the only way to explain this?" Mac paced the hallway.

"Remember, he didn't die from the knife wound. He died from a ventricle bursting before the knife could do any actual fatal damage."

"Was he trying to relieve pressure in his chest or something? Also, why did he bring the knife with him out to the football field while wearing a Viking helmet? He was obviously celebrating a win, but with a steak knife? Seems rather odd." Mac asked.

"He could have just been acting silly." Vince said. "The steak knife as a silly weapon of a Viking celebrating a victory? Something just doesn't add up."

"Someone could have forced the knife into his chest using his own hand. Still, why would he be out on the field, around a bunch of kids, with a knife sticking out of his chest? We obviously have more work to do. I'll head back to the Gonzalez household and see if I can't get us some more answers."

CHAPTER THIRTEEN

Mac drove back to Batavia. His mind wandered to the last case where he'd dealt with a young person being the victim. Though Gainor was in his early twenties and out of school, he still had his whole life ahead of him. Mac sometimes felt that he should seek out some form of therapy to deal with situations like this. He still had a job to do, he couldn't let a flood of negative emotion and grief take hold. There were some supports in the CPD, but not nearly enough to deal with the trauma and intensity of situations many people like himself found themselves in. Being a police officer had its perks, but also lasting effects after the job was long gone.

Many cops with long careers don't live long after the job is over. The post-traumatic stress can take hold and grip former police officers. It was probably a mixture of what they did, maybe situations they could have handled better and, of course, the awful crimes they had to deal with and stop. Mac limped and needed the use of a cane for the types of crime he stopped. He had chronic pain which served as harsh reminder that he too may need more help than he let on. He truly needed Millie in his life.

Mac pulled onto the dark street. He decided not to arouse Papa Bear Gonzalez this time and parked further down the street. He didn't want the headlights or sound of the car door closing to arouse Gonzalez, guaranteeing that he wouldn't open the door again. Maybe someone else would open the door this time. Maybe even Lacey, the girl he needed to talk to.

Before he reached the walkway to the front door, he heard sobbing from somewhere beyond the house. It was closer to the dense woods that made up the boundary line of the Gonzalez backyard. Mac used his cane and cut a path between the Gonzalez house and their next door neighbor's house.

More sobbing. Louder this time.

Mac drew closer to the source.

A girl in a cheerleader uniform walked slowly

from the wooded area and over to the Gonzalez back patio and double door entry.

Mac stopped and ducked behind the air conditioning fan next door. He didn't want to startle her and didn't want to give away his position.

The cheerleader stopped on the patio and sat at a picnic table. She continued crying, with her head on the table and her shoulders rising and falling with each mournful sob.

Mac figured he should introduce himself and get this over with. She was already upset. How much more upset could she get if an ex-cop walked up to ask her a few questions?

He noticed there were barrels around the picnic table. Wooden barrels. And empty bottles lined up on the table. Wine bottles? Perhaps the Gonzalez family made their own wine?

Illinois was not known for its vast expanse of vineyards and valleys akin to California's Napa.

It was Festival of the Wine weekend...maybe the Gonzalez family were vendors?

"Lacey?" Mac spoke softly and tried to walk in her line of sight when she raised her head from the table.

"Wha—who is that?!" Lacey looked toward Mac, her eyes peeking over the wine bottles.

"I am a police officer. I just wanted to talk to you about Coach Gainor."

"Leave me alone!"

Suddenly a flash ignited into Mac's field of vision from the direction of the tree line at the back of the yard.

A fire ball flew towards Mac. Maybe a Molotov cocktail?

Mac fell to the ground and covered up. When he looked up, the flames of the presumed alcohol-based incendiary projectile were nowhere to be found.

No Molotov and no Lacey.

CHAPTER FOURTEEN

Mac reached his feet and scanned the area. He pulled his cellphone out and used the flashlight. It wasn't very bright, but it just felt like the right thing to do. The cheerleader vanished and a fire ball flew towards him, then dissipated almost as fast as he saw it fly through the air! He expected the dry leaves of autumn blanketing the backyard grass to ignite.

And nothing happened.

Mac decided to at least search the tree line of the woods behind the Gonzalez home. Going into the woods didn't seem like that great of an idea, as the darkness did little to comfort the veteran ex-cop.

"Creepy woods on a windy fall evening. Not exactly the best way to start the Festival weekend.

And, what the hell happened?" Mac muttered to himself and walked to the back of the yard near the trees.

The bark of a tree met his gaze. He looked left and right. Nothing, just more trees. Bark. And the occasional hoot of an owl somewhere above.

Being a city guy, Mac didn't have much experience with nature and especially nature at night. He never went camping—ever. He went to Cubs games and played on his city block that was always well-lit and well-monitored by the parents on porches, having a few beers on a nice summer evening. Going into the woods by himself, in this situation, didn't seem like the best idea.

Mac had a hard time believing what just happened. He stepped back from the woods and listened again for the crunching of leaves under someone's foot. Again, the owl hooted.

Suddenly the floodlights on the back of the house lit up the backyard. Mac turned around and put his forearm to shield his eyes from the light.

"What are you doing back there?" Mr. Gonzalez yelled.

"Sir, I am sorry. I heard your daughter crying back here and I just thought I would ask her a few questions. I didn't want to disturb you again." Mac walked closer to Lacey's Dad, who stood on the patio next to the barrels.

Mr. Gonzalez walked back into the house.

Mac shook his head. Perhaps he was checking to see if Lacey was home?

"Where is she?! She was here. She was in her room!" Mr. Gonzalez walked back out, now clearly upset.

"Sir, I think she went into the woods." Mac put his palms up as if to calm her father.

"That damn Dennis kid. I told her I didn't like that kid."

"Dennis?

"Yes, there is a clearing not too far into the woods where she and her friends hang out. She's probably just there with Dennis. I will handle it from here. You can leave. I don't want her to talking to any cops." Mr. Gonzalez walked back into the house. "Just leave us alone!"

"Mr. Gonzalez, I just need to ask her some questions about a murder. It is very important that I talk to her. Let me help you find her!" Mac walked onto the back patio.

Mr. Gonzalez walked back out carrying a large torch flashlight and blew right past Mac. "Lacey!"

Mac decided to follow, despite the fact that Mr. Gonzalez clearly didn't want him there.

Into the woods they went.

CHAPTER FIFTEEN

Mr. Gonzalez didn't seem to worry about the fact that it was late in the evening and the woods were creepy and unsettling. He marched to the so-called clearing he spoke of, his pace frantic. Mac did his best to keep up and not rely too much on his cane. He just limped quickly.

"Lacey!" Mr. Gonzalez yelled.

The trees seemed to multiply the further they hiked. Mac looked up to check if he could see the stars or the moon. It just looked dark above him. His phone flashlight and Mr. Gonzalez's torch helped him make sense of his surroundings. Flashes of horror movies about witches in the woods that were popular in his youth caused Mac's heart to beat harder. The sound of crunching leaves and breaking sticks crackled in his ears.

The woods felt claustrophobic. His breaths became shallow. His forehead broke out in a sweat. His heart pumped harder and faster.

Mr. Gonzalez stopped. "Here's the clearing."

"Not exactly a clearing." Mac followed but flashed his phone's light at a stone bulging out from the leafy ground. Mac knelt down and cleared away the leaves. The stone looked manipulated. It looked like an engraving.

"Oh yeah, those things." Mr. Gonzalez seemed to ignore Mac's find.

"You mean a gravestone. This is a tiny cemetery. Look over there." Mac pointed to a few more, small, rounded, and very old headstones. They were crooked and not put into the ground with much care. The two men stood on the bones of people long dead.

"Just some old gravestones. What is the big deal? The bigger deal is the fact that Lacey is missing." Mr. Gonzalez walked up to the only tree that breached the perimeter of the clearing. It had a hollowed out trunk. He poured the light from his torch into the tree trunk.

Mac looked over his shoulder. There were carvings on the inside of the trunk. Strange symbols that he'd never seen before and one very familiar: a heart with an arrow struck through it. He couldn't make out the names underneath it, as they were blotted out...actually burnt out.

Mac officially contracted a case of the creeps.

"Yes, we really need to find her. We can try that Dennis kid's number and even pay a visit to his house. I really can help you, Mr. Gonzalez," Mac took a deep breath, trying to mask his fears.

"Lacey left her phone in her room. She is probably with Dennis. I will try him back at the house."

"Good plan." Mac let out a sigh, happy to be leaving the creepy graveyard in the middle of the woods.

The walk back felt much shorter than the walk in. Mr. Gonzalez walked into the house through the patio doors without another word.

The events of the past half hour ran through Mac's mind. A flashing fireball that dissipated as quickly as it flew towards him and the near-immediate disappearance of a cheerleader. A young man's heart basically bursting in his chest, causing him to die and possibly plunge a knife into his own chest.

Mac began to think that the problems weren't natural.

Time to call Millie.

CHAPTER SIXTEEN

"Millie, I am sorry to wake you." Mac paced the patio and examined the wine bottles on the picnic table.

"You didn't wake me. I'm just laying around watching TV. I can't really fall asleep for some reason. What is happening?" Millie sounded more tired than she let on.

"How's Beck?"

"Oh dear, she is fine. She is happily asleep. She needs to slow down, she gulps down alcohol like water."

"You have tacos?"

"Ha. Yes, yes, we did. She insisted on it."

"Too funny. Speaking of funny, I had some funny things happen to me but in the strange way, not the comedic way. Gainor's heart basically burst in his chest and the examiner doesn't think he died from the knife wound. Also, a cheerleader from Batavia High literally disappeared on me as I approached her, right as a ball of flame that I thought was a Molotov cocktail came flying out of the woods." Mac kept his voice low. Mr. Gonzalez hadn't come out yet.

"Whoa, slow down. You want me to join you?"

"Yes, I would. What do you think is going on?"

"Honestly, it seems like there could be some things I should check out with you. You say the kid disappeared after a ball of flame flew towards you?"

"Yes, ma'am. When there is something I really can't explain, I just take a wild guess that maybe you can explain it. Since, you know, you are a wi —" Mac put the phone down as Mr. Gonzalez walked back out of the house. "Any luck reaching Dennis?"

"No luck on reaching Dennis. I'm sure she will show up. I will wait before I bring in more cops on this. She's had a rough night, I am sure she will be back soon." Mr. Gonzalez walked back into the house and slammed the patio doors shut.

He really didn't like cops at all.

"Mr. Gonzalez. Wait!" Mac yelled.

Mac put the phone back up to his ear. "Sorry, Millie. The cheerleader's dad is not cooperative."

"Think he may have something to do with what's going on?" Millie asked.

"Honestly, I don't think so. I just don't think he likes cops very much. He really doesn't want me around."

"Text me the address of the house you are at and I will meet you there."

"Yes, just drive to the block before this one and we can avoid him. Then we go check out the creepy cemetery I was just in."

"Oh, great fun. I will be sure to bring my wand."

"See you soon." Mac ended the call and scanned the backyard once more for evidence of a Molotov.

Mr. Gonzalez shut the outside light off. Guess it was time for him to go.

He walked the side of the house to the street, heading in the direction of his car when Vince called.

"Vincey, what ya got for me?"

"When Gainor's parent's came here to ID the body, we made sure to ask if Dennis had any heart problems, you know, a murmur or any other irregularities and they said no. Whatever caused his heart to burst was not inherently biological. Also, we checked out his phone and he had a smartwatch that recorded his heartbeat. He had a healthy heart rate. So yeah, we hit a wall there." Vince's voice sounded tired.

"Hmm...yeah I don't know. I hit a wall over here, too. No one is answering the door." Mac couldn't explain what was happening to Vince. He didn't have to know if any sort of magic was involved and, besides, Millie was on her way.

"Okay, I would just call it a night. I will head there tomorrow morning and interview the kid. No worries. Bye." Vince ended the call.

Mac walked to end of the street and opened his car door. He couldn't shake the creepy feeling that overtook him as he and Mr. Gonzalez ventured into the woods. Something was very wrong.

Something wicked lurked in those woods.

CHAPTER SEVENTEEN

Millie pulled her black sedan nose to nose with Mac's blue sedan on a sleepy block in Batavia, Illinois. Her exhaustion dissipated with the excitement of another mystery to solve with Mac O'Malley. She smiled when she saw him. She loved the man and was happy to help. She made sure her wand was tucked into her jacket pocket as she felt she would need it this evening.

"Hello, sir." Millie exited her vehicle and gave Mac a hug.

"I am so glad to see you." Mac squeezed her a bit harder than usual.

"Well, I was thinking on the way here about the fireball you saw. That is Magic 101. It is one of the first things magic users learn: how to send out sparking fireballs from our wand. It's more for the use of light than it is for starting fires, which explains why it disappeared so quickly." Millie pulled back and squeezed Mac's shoulders.

"How about the kid disappearing? I mean, I suppose she could have run away. It just seemed like there wasn't that much time from when I ducked and covered to when I peeked out to see if it was really a Molotov or not. We have to examine the woods a bit more. Can you light the way for us with your fireflies spell you used at Halliburton's house?" Mac asked.

"Yes, of course. What is in the woods again?"

"Yes, sorry, it was a clearing with some grave-stones and a tree with a hollowed out trunk. The inside of the trunk had some weird carvings in it. The whole thing just gives me the creeps."

"That does sound creepy. Let's go check it out."

Mac and Millie walked back to the tree line, but stayed a few houses away from the Gonzalez house-hold to try and cover their movements.

They made their way into the woods. Mac said, "Lets' stick to the yard line here until we get to the Gonzalez house. Then, it is just hard right and a straight shot to the clearing. I think."

"Any more news on Coach Gainor?"

"Yes, his family said he had no history of heart

disease or any irregularities. So, no preexisting condition for his heart to burst."

"This is very strange. Honestly, Mac, I don't think there any spells that cause heart explosions. Still, I am glad you asked for my help. Besides, after what happened to you at Swedish Days you need me to protect you."

"Ha! You are totally right. I do need you to protect me. I admit it. No pride here." Mac laughed.

The temperature on this particular fall evening dropped to near freezing. Millie now regretted leaving her cozy warm bed to traipse around the woods with Mac.

"Okay, here we go. It's a right turn from here." Mac pointed with his cane.

"Let's get in a bit further and then I will light the way."

"Sounds like a plan. Do you hear the owl?" Mac panicked. "What was that?"

"Mac, relax. No, I don't hear an owl or anything. You are just spooked. *Fireflies*." Millie pulled out her wand. The tip of her wand glowed orange and tiny sparks of light filled the woodsy air around them.

Mac made sure to look up the trees for the owl. No owl. The light from Millie's wand showed the rough bark of the trees and the brown, yellow, and orange leaves of the ground cover. He felt better now that visibility improved. The woods were beautiful and not as creepy in the right light.

He led Millie to the clearing. "Here we are and watch your step. The gravestones are scattered around and you can trip on them easily."

"Did you trip on one?"

"I honestly didn't."

"Right." Millie said sarcastically.

"For reals. I didn't."

"Again, I believe you." Millie smirked in the orange glow. "Okay, what are we doing here?"

"I don't know. Isn't there some way you can trace magic or something? Take a look at the tree trunk." Mac pointed at the hollowed out tree.

Millie raised her wand and concentrated the orange light on the inside of the trunk.

"Found something Mac."

"What? It's not like Satan shit or anything is it?"

"There is a door at the bottom of this trunk."

"A door?"

"Yes."

"Oh, great, so it probably leads to a pit like the one in *Silence of the Lambs*."

"You could use a drink like Mom. Come on, hero cop. Let's open it up." Millie pointed down.

CHAPTER EIGHTEEN

Mac looked around the graveyard clearing and he noticed many more crooked gravestones and bulging grave markers now that Millie's wand lit the area. He reluctantly walked over to the hollow tree trunk.

"Did you say a door?"

"Yes, Mac. A door. You are really freaked out, aren't you? Help me lift it up." Millie stepped out and grabbed a small rusty chain.

Mac grabbed the chain with Millie and pulled. The heavy wooden object moved with their combined might.

"This is more like a sewer cap than a door! Sheesh!" Mac pulled a bit harder.

Billowing dust sprayed through the air.

"It's open!" Millie said.

The couple dropped the chain and looked into the hole they just uncovered. Millie bent down and sent more fireflies into the opening below.

There was a narrow staircase that led down.

"I feel like we did this underground tunnel thing already at Geneva High School." Mac rubbed his leg.

"We definitely did. This may not be a tunnel. Let's get down there and see where it leads. Maybe the kid is down here?"

"Or we could just see if Lacey comes home in the morning?"

"Mac, come on down here." Millie descended the narrow earthen steps.

Mac gripped his cane and made his way down the steps behind her. This didn't seem like a good idea.

"Whoa. Mac, I think I know what this might be."

Mac made his way down to the dirt floor. The room had shelves with jars everywhere. The walls had wooden planks that barely kept the earth from collapsing and filling the room.

"Is that a charger cord for a phone?" Mac pointed at a white cord on the ground.

"Looks like this place has been used recently. A little cauldron as well, probably for potion-making—

also used recently." Millie examined a small cast-iron bowl.

"How would they see in here? Oh wait, I see: there is a little generator in here. Wow, quite the little set up." Mac jabbed his cane into the red and black gas generator.

"Mac, look at this picture. Think this is who is buried above us ? Or I guess next to us from where we are standing." Millie handed Mac a small square picture frame.

Mac examined the black and white picture. It was a group of young women. No smiles. There were three of them varying in age, from about early twenties to maybe twelve or so. Mac removed the back of the frame and searched for any mark of who they were.

"The Jurgensen family. Interesting. Must be sisters I suppose? Did they hang out down here or what?" Mac asked.

"Mac, now I don't want you to freak out. In magical history, the Jurgensen sisters were put on trial for witchcraft and executed. This could very well be their hideout and place of rest."

Mac didn't say a word. He just stared at the picture and took a deep breath. The smell of dirt and musk filled his nose. The place just smelled old as another indicator of its actual decrepit state. Dank and moldy, practically a tomb....

"Mac? At least we know the kids come here. We could just stake the place out and see who returns."

"If the kids ever return. What if the Jurgensen sisters haunt this place and took out their revenge on Lacey and this Dennis kid? We should get far away from here."

"Mac. Ghosts aren't real."

"This coming from a witch who flies on a broom and basically has superpowers?! Tell me more about the Jurgensen sisters."

"What else is there to say? They were magic users and they were persecuted for it. That's why things are kept pretty locked down and separate. We have the Constables and the Coven to keep things in check, so terrible things, like happened to the sisters, don't happen to people like me and my family."

"Makes sense. I'm sorry." Mac rubbed his eyes.

"Yes, the witches won't haunt children. They were children themselves." Millie frowned.

"So sorry...you are right. It has been a long night. A really long night. Anything else we can use for clues in here?"

Leaves floated down in front of the stairs, followed by a large booming sound.

"Oh no!" Mac jumped to the stairs.

The heavy wooden door closed. Someone shut them in.

Mac and Millie were trapped in a witch hideout in the middle of the woods.

CHAPTER NINETEEN

"Oh, that's not good. We can't be stuck down here, right?" Mac lifted his cane and tried to push the door upwards.

"I can use my magic and push the door open. No problem. Get back, Mac." Millie pointed the wand up the steep stairwell to the door.

Mac stepped behind Millie to avoid being hit with whatever spell was about to be cast. His heart hadn't stopped racing since they entered the clearing and, of course, found this cubby hole hideout for creepy kids.

"Repulse!" Millie yelled. Her arm shook with the force of the spell that shot out from her wand.

The concussive blast of the spell blew Mac's hair back. He felt a rush of air on his face.

Millie lowered her wand and examined the door at the top of the stairs.

"We free to go, Mills?" Mac coughed and covered his mouth. Dust and dirt filled the air around them.

"Apparently not. Wow. That is one of my strongest spells. The cubby hole door didn't even budge! Hmm. Well, Mac, unless there is a building or something resting on top of that piece of wood, there is no other reason for the door not opening other than a counter spell of some kind. We can confirm we are definitely dealing with a magic-user. Be sure to take pics of those jars on the shelves too. We have to figure out some possible combinations of potions that could be made and used in this tiny cauldron." Mille wiped the dust from her face, crossed her arms, and sported a contemplative look.

"Okay, Mills. That is all fine and dandy, but we can't get the bad guys unless we get out of here." Mac still took pictures of the whole subterranean room with his phone, complying with Millie's directive.

"Let's put our heads together here. We could see if my spell moves the door at all. I will do it again and you can just jam your cane up there. Maybe I can move the door enough for you to stick the cane in between it and the ground."

"Ah, yes, then use the cane to pry the door open! Wait. Will I be safe from the spell or will my head be crushed or all my hair be ripped out of my head?"

"I mean, Mac, you do already have a small bald spot, so maybe the spell will help speed the balding process along?" Millie threw her hands up.

"I do not have a bald spot! Wait, do I have a bald spot?" Mac felt sheepish.

Millie just gestured an inch with her index finger and thumb.

"A tiny one? Whatever. Let's just get out of this horrible place already!" Mac stepped in front of Millie and raised his cane to the ceiling door.

"I promise I will just hit the door. I am going to try a stronger, more concentrated spell. You may feel some force, but it will just be like a strong wind. Okay?"

"Yes. Do it."

"Don't tell me what to do." Millie stepped closer to the stairs and Mac and pointed her wand up.

"Yikes." Mac laughed and gripped the cane tight, ready to push it up.

"Repulse Maximo!" Millie used the power of concussive enchantment on the door once more.

Mac pushed and felt the door give way from

Millie's more powerful spell. He used all his might to push the cane between the ground and the door.

"I got it, Mills. It worked! Help me push the door open." Mac grunted as he tried to pry the door open. He stopped and let go. His cane scraped the ceiling of the small hideout.

"You did it, Mac. We have some leverage now. Gonna use the spell one more time and that should do the trick. Hang in there. Repulse Maximo!" Millie yelled the spell.

Mac's cane fell to the ground. He coughed and waved the dust and dirt away from his face.

"We are good to go, Mac."

"Did we even need the cane?"

"Yes. It broke the seal of the blocking spell. Sometimes, it takes a combination of the real and magical to get out of jams."

"So, what you are saying is we are a great combination."

"Um. Sure." Millie climbed the steps.

Mac smiled and shook his head, then bent down and recovered his cane.

CHAPTER TWENTY

Mac and Millie were both glad to be out in the chilly autumn air. Millie examined the tree trunk and the door.

"What caused the door problem?"

"A simple sealing spell: a decently strong, yet simple one. Like, maybe Magic 102."

"Fascinating. Do you think you can convince Mr. Gonzalez to talk to me? He won't cooperate." Mac began the walk back to the Gonzalez's backyard.

"I can probably do that, but we may not even have to bother him. You said Lacey and Dennis were the names of the kids? I don't know why I didn't think of this earlier." Millie traded her wand for the phone in her jacket pocket.

"What are you thinking?"

"There is a register the Coven updates weekly. A register of magic users. I can check for Lacey Gonzalez and for a kid with the first name of Dennis in Batavia. There isn't that many of us. If they are able to do potions and sealing spells, they are on the register automagically. Ha see what I did there?"

"Millie, that really wasn't funny, but why is it making me smile like a total idiot?" Mac shook his head again.

"No Lacey in Batavia's register. Aha! There is a sixteen-year-old named Dennis Gainor on the list. Address is not far from here, right near Fabyan Parkway." Millie smiled and showed Mac the screen of her phone.

"Did you say Gainor?"

"Oh wow. Yes. Gainor."

"Let's roll there right now. The kid may be related to the victim! Is that register like Santa's naughty and nice list or something? Like it generates by itself? I mean, Santa can't really sort all the kids like that. So many kids, you know? Literally at this point, billions." Mac really focused his energy on his words.

"Mac! Santa? Seriously."

"Why wouldn't I be serious?" Mac looked Millie right in the eyes.

412 FABYAN. A nice ranch house, with white shutters and blue siding. The Gainor household. The lights were out. There was no one around. Mac and Millie stood next to the crooked mailbox beside the curb.

"Well, do we just knock on the door or what?" Mac asked.

"Let me see what I can do." Millie pulled out her wand and waved it.

"What are you doing?"

"He's here. They're in the basement." Millie walked to the side of the ranch.

"How do you know?"

"The lights are on in the windows near the ground." Millie laughed.

"So, what was with the wand waving thing?"

"I was messing with you." Millie turned and stopped to let Mac catch up.

"Real funny tonight, aren't you? We gonna knock on the window?"

"No, I am going to send them a message with my

wand. I am going to use a spell that will send my voice to them."

"Ha, yeah right. Fool me once, fool me twice."

"I am not messing with you this time. For real, Officer O'Malley."

Mac and Millie bent down to look in the window.

Wood-paneled walls, brown couches, and orange carpet denoted a style stuck in the 1970s. A girl in a cheerleader uniform lay on a couch, asleep. Dennis Gainor played video games sitting on the floor, an energy drink open next to him. He was dressed in a black hoodie with a skull icon on the back of it.

"There he is and that is Lacey. Same outfit she wore earlier," Mac said.

"Dennis. Please don't be alarmed. I am at the window behind you. I am a magic user like you and I just want to talk to you." Millie spoke into the tip of her wand then waved it toward the window and Dennis, who still played his video game with intensity and blissful ignorance of what was happening around him.

He suddenly dropped the controller. The teenaged boy slowly turned his head in fear, probably in disbelief that a woman's voice just burst into his ears and told him to look behind him at the window.

"You officially freaked the kid out. Great job, Mills."

"What is he doing? Oh, don't let him fool you. Oh no. Don't even think about it." Millie stood up from her crouching position at the window.

"What's happening? What is he doing?" Mac watched Dennis shake his head at the window.

"Mac. Stand back."

The lights in the basement turned off.

"Oh hell no. He isn't going to fight you. He will get his ass kicked! Get him, Mills." Mac heeded Millie's warning and stepped back toward his car on the street.

From the window, a mist seeped out like that of a genie emerging from a lamp.

"Mac, don't look at this mist. Shut your eyes!"

"What about you? Mills?"

This mist formed into a large shape akin to the Ghost of Christmas Future. Hooded, tall, with a deathly look. It could have just been Mac's imagination, but it seemed to form into a seemingly sinister, iconic shape.

Mac forgot to shut his eyes. He couldn't quell his curiosity for the supernatural phenomena on display in front of him. Suddenly, the visual recall of Gainor's dead body on the ball field filled his vision along with the kid that he couldn't save all those years in Chicago. A great doubt filled his heart. A creeping feel of despair slithered like a constrictor on his chest. He fell to the ground.

"Mac! Protector!" Millie yelled.

The immense pressure on his chest alleviated. He felt better with Millie's spell.

Millie ran to help him off the lawn.

"What the heck was that?" Mac asked.

"The kid is into some bad magic. Darkness spells that reflect typical teenage angst, but can manifest and cause despair in those around them. I'm glad you are okay. They disappeared and my guess is he used— "

"Instant travel magic like what got us in trouble over the summer. Now what do we do?"

"We have to go 272 and see Grandma Jo."

CHAPTER TWENTY-ONE

Mac and Millie drove separately to 272 WitchHazel Drive and the childhood home of one magical Millie Paderson.

It was late. They would have to wake Beck and Hank up, but Grandma Jo rarely slept anymore. She was awake in the basement apartment reading a bloody murder mystery. She loved to read and the books that kept her attention and kept her awake at night were not exactly easy reads. She loved a good thrill. She would probably enjoy the story of Mac and Millie's evening.

She could definitely help.

Millie hit the button for the large, iron gate and proceeded into the driveway. The yellow house with gothic spires actually looked pretty cool at night with cool accent lighting up the main turret of the house. She did really like her home. Sometimes, the people therein were a little kooky—namely Becca.

Millie parked and Mac was right behind her.

"Here we go. I mean, we may be able to get in without waking up Mom and Dad. I have a key and we just need to head to the basement door." Millie said.

"Okay, how can Grandma Jo help us? Is she like, a Grand Witch or something?"

"Haha, well she is a very powerful magic user. She also knows potions forwards and backwards and will know what Dennis was mixing in the hideout. You have the picture, right?"

"Yes, I have the pic in my phone. We also have the baby cauldron. I stuffed it in my pocket." Mac took the small coffee-mug sized potion mixer out of his jacket pocket.

Millie walked up to the green door and turned the key. The light in the front hall flooded the bushes and landscaping next to the door. Before Millie could open the door, Hank did.

"Millie. What is going on?" Hank asked.

"Hank! I am so surprised you made it down faster than me!" Becca walked down the stairs after Hank. She was dressed in pink pajamas and a robe.

Hank shook his head.

"Let's face it, he *is* super slow." Becca stood next to him.

"I beat you down, here didn't I?!" Hank yelled.

"Guys! Stop." Milie sighed. "Sorry to wake you—we just have to talk to Grandma. She's probably awake still."

"Oh, okay. Yeah, let's head down there. Hi Mac." Becca said.

"Hello! Sorry it's so late." Mac followed Millie to the basement door.

They walked down the carpeted stairs to the basement. A lamp was on and, sure enough, Grandma Joan sat in a recliner reading through a book with a knife on the cover and large font denoting an author hack named Michaels.

"Grandma Jo? It's Millie." Millie waved to her elder.

"Oh, jeez I didn't even hear you guys."

"Must be really into the book, huh?" Mac asked.

"Not really. The author's just okay. What are you doing here so late?" She smiled, glad to have the company. Grandma Joan didn't look like a woman in her eighties. Her hair hadn't turned gray and she didn't have many wrinkles. She looked much younger than her actual age. For a woman who gave birth to six children, one of whom is more than a handful—Becca—she looked fantastic.

"We have a few questions to ask you. Needless to say, it's been a strange night. We know you are the master at potions, baking, anything that requires ingredients." Millie sat down on the couch next to the recliner.

"Well, I just follow directions mostly." Grandma Jo laughed.

"We both know that's not true, Mother." Becca interjected. "You fiddle around endlessly and throw half of your stuff away if it's not perfect."

"What can I help you with?"

"A young, new magic-user is fiddling around and experimenting with dark magic and we found a weird underground hideout in the middle of the woods. We think there may be a connection with the dark magic and the death of a Geneva football coach," Millie said.

"Yes, I heard about the coach. A young man, too. So sad."

"Here is what we found in the hideout. We took pictures." Mac showed Jo his phone.

"Hmm, let me have that." Joan grabbed the phone.

"No problem. Any thoughts? We also have the

cauldron the kid mixed the stuff in. Would that help?" Mac asked.

"Hmm. These are the ingredients for a love potion. Love potions have been banned for quite some time. It's against the magical laws of the Coven to use any magic to make people fall in love with them. They are dangerous. Extremely dangerous."

"What happens if someone is given a love potion, Grandma?"

"Whoever drinks the potion becomes obsessed with the person who gave it to them. They basically don't leave the person alone." Grandma used her fingers to zoom in on the picture of the ingredients on the hideout's shelving.

"So, that's all that happens? Just intense infatuation?" Mac asked.

"Maybe I should give Hank some," Becca said.

"Mom." Millie shot her mother a dirty look.

"Well, it becomes too much for the person who both gives the potion and the one who receives it. Also—now I don't necessarily know if this is true, but this is a rumor I heard from downstate in the town where I grew up. If the person who drinks the potion breaks another person's heart, like a spouse or significant other, the person who drank the potion will die." Grandma Joan lowered the phone and stared at Mac and Millie.

"You mean, their heart will literally break? The person who drank the potion?" Mac rubbed his chin. His eyes were wide.

"Yes, I suppose that is one way that it could happen. Yes. I heard that it causes a lot of pain and pressure in the chest, as if your heart will burst. Nasty stuff. Worse than any book I have read and I have read some gruesome books."

"That is how Coach Gainor died then. Lacey gave him the love potion that Dennis made or they made together. Misty Rigby's heart was broken and it caused Coach Gainor's heart to burst. He stuck the knife into his chest to relieve the pressure in his chest. He got excited that the team won which caused his heart to beat harder. He was probably desperate at that point." Mac paced the Berber carpet and walked around the pool table at the bottom of the stairs.

"Thanks Grandma." Millie gave her Grandmother a big hug. Grandmothers like Joan were to be cherished.

"Love you too, Millie." Grandma smiled.

"Mac, we can't let Vince know any of this. We have to call in the Constables on this one. I will get them over to the graveyard to keep watch. We should meet them there. We can call Marie's boyfriend, Ben. I don't think Dennis is aware of the Coven yet. He has been reckless with his magic and experimenting with dark magic. Probably researched the crap on the internet." Millie walked back to the base of the stairs.

Mac nodded. "Okay, let's get the Constables on this one. You are right: this is one murder that will not be solved in the traditional sense."

CHAPTER TWENTY-TWO

Mac and Millie took Mac's blue car and headed back to the woods behind the Gonzalez house. Ben the Constable was waiting for them on the corner, well away from the Gonzalez household.

Millie opened the car door. "Hey Ben."

"Hey Millie. Hey Mac." Ben nodded his head. He looked a bit sheepish, probably from the last time they encountered each other and Ben tried to stop Millie and Marie's rescue of a hexed Mac.

"Ben, don't worry about it! You were doing your job!" Millie patted his shoulder.

"Thanks Millie. The kid is definitely not aware of the Coven or trace magic. We were alerted to essence of hummingbird being used here earlier.

They are already back in the area. I think they are in the wooded area you talked about.”

“Maybe the kid wanted to check and see if we escaped? Did he not see us at the house?” Mac looked at Millie.

“Help! Help!” A girl screamed from the woods.

Ben and Millie turned to the woods first.

“I’ll stay here and keep watch from the front! Go! It has to be Lacey!” Mac yelled and stayed in his car.

Millie didn’t think she would ever encounter someone using dark magic so close to home. People just didn’t do it anymore. Gone were the days of using magic to bend the real world to your advantage, in whatever way possible.

“I know where she most likely is! Follow me, Ben.” Millie ran behind the corner house and to the tree line of the woods. She loved to run in short bursts. She was faster than Ben. Much faster.

Millie didn’t even bother to wait for Ben. She ran to the Gonzalez back yard and took a sharp right into the woods.

“Help!” The girl’s voice sounded from right in front of her.

The girl ran past Millie and to the backyard.

Millie followed. "Lacey? Are you okay? I'm here to help. What's the matter?"

Lacey, still in her cheerleader regalia, fell to the cold grass of her backyard. She pointed behind Millie and to the woods. "Look out!"

A ball of flame flew toward Millie's back.

"Get down!" Lacey yelled.

Millie dove for the ground at Lacey's white sneakers. "Don't worry, I got this."

She rolled to her back and fired an icy blue streak from her wand into the trees. The spell caused bark to fly from a tree and into the yard.

"He is insane! I ran as fast as I could!" Lacey panted. "He's like a sorcerer or something, like some Dungeons and Dragons shit!"

"Get in your house and stay in there. I can handle it from here." Millie stood up and faced the woods.

"I'm going. Keep him away from here, please!" Lacey ran to the patio door.

Ben finally caught up to Millie. "What's going on?"

"He's in the woods. Light the area up, please." Millie readied her wand and entered the woods. The chilly air penetrated her lungs with each inhale. The crunch of leaves and twigs sounded louder and louder with each careful step into the woods.

"Torch!" Ben yelled. A giant tongue of flame grew from the tip of this wand, then detached from his wand. Like a flare, it hovered just below the tree line in the woods and gave them a clear view of the trees leading to the clearing and graveyard.

The graveyard was closer than Millie thought.

"Dennis! Stand down! There are two of us and one of you!" Millie moved her head from side to side as Ben's torch helped light her path.

"He's still in here, probably just hiding behind a tree. Or maybe in that hideout? Hiding?" Ben looked around parallel to Millie.

"No, he wouldn't be in there, would he? Well, maybe he wants to destroy the evidence..."

Upon entry into the clearing, the hollowed out tree burst and cracked in half, a vertical split right down the middle. A huge branch fell between Millie and Ben.

"Holy hell!" Ben yelled.

Fire burst from the hideout inside the tree, just between the two fallen halves of the trunk. It was as if a phoenix had risen from the ashes in the middle of the tree.

"Ben, don't get distracted!" Mille took her eyes off the flame sucking up oxygen from the hideout.

A ball of flame flew towards him from the trees next to the clearing. He ducked and the fiery spell flew right past Millie's face.

She fired a volley of the same icy blue counter spell back at Dennis.

The teenager walked into the clearing and ducked down behind a tombstone. "Leave me alone!"

"Dennis, we know you are scared but we can help you with your magic powers. You just have to stop slinging fireballs at everyone!" Millie yelled.

Ben jumped over the fallen, splintered tree and pointed his wand at the crooked tombstone Dennis hid behind. He stood next to Millie, his body tense.

"I will freeze him and you disarm him. Ready?" Millic whispered.

"Ready!"

Time seemed to slow. down. The mist and smoke that earlier spewed from the window billowed out from behind the tombstone. The fire crackled and danced. The wind suddenly howled and leaves fell into courtyard.

Millie made her move. She jumped over the tree,

now turned log, and ran to the right side of the tombstone.

At the same time, Ben ran to the left side.

The smoke formed into a shape once more, forming above Dennis and the tombstone.

"Don't look at it Ben!" Millie fired at Dennis—he didn't anticipate the bull rush.

Her icy spell petrified Dennis.

"Disarm!" Ben yelled.

Dennis dropped the wand or, rather, it fell from his slowly opening hand after Millie's freezing spell took effect. He stayed crouched behind the tombstone.

"The effects of my spell won't last long. Better bind his hands. Let's bring him to Lacey's house and get to the bottom of this." Millie wiped actual sweat from her forehead.

The smoke dissipated. Gone with the wind.

CHAPTER TWENTY-THREE

Mac joined Millie, Ben, Dennis (a cuffed Dennis at that), and Lacey in her backyard.

"What happened, Lacey?" Mac asked.

"Wait, Ben. You made sure Mr. Gonzalez is asleep, right?" Millie looked at Ben, her expression somewhat panicked.

"He won't remember anything from the last twelve hours. All set." Ben nodded.

"Again, what happened?"

"It all started a week or so ago. I was over at Dennis' house. I went to have dinner at with him and his family. After that dinner, his older brother Tim became really strange towards me. He started calling me and talking to me. Like he liked...*really* liked me. Like, wanted me."

Mac and Millie exchanged looks.

"So, he basically fell in love with you? Did you like him at all?" Millie asked.

"Yes, she did!" Dennis yelled. "She loved him!"

"Whoa, Dennis, we want Lacey's side of the story first. You shut it." Mac pointed a finger at him.

"I mean, I had a crush on Tim I admit, but I never thought it would seriously happen. He just wanted to be around me. All the time. I got a bit freaked out, you know?" Lacey rubbed her cheeks, still damp mascara tracked tears.

"So, his behavior became very odd." Millie nodded.

"Yes, I knew he had a girlfriend and everything. Also, I'm only sixteen and it's just wrong to be with a twenty-three-year-old or whatever he was," Lacey explained.

"Lacey, you said you were having dinner at the Gainor's home. Are you friends with Dennis?" Mac asked.

"Yes, we grew up together. Our families are close. And then I heard that Tim died. I just wanted to grieve and the things got real weird and Dennis became really strange. I suddenly appeared in his basement and he wouldn't let me go. Then we came back here and I finally was able to get away from him when he said he needed to check something in the woods. I thought he was going to kill me. There's a creepy graveyard in there. Well, you know."

"Tell us more about the dinner with the Gainors. Tell us every detail: including what you ate, drank, etcetera." Mac sucked in a sharp breath, trying his damnedest not to pressure her. "Can you do that?"

"Well, my Dad brought some of our wine we import from Mexico. Tim actually loved the wine. Then we sat down to eat."

"Is that what these barrels are? Wine? And you guys bottle the wine here?" Mac asked.

"Yes, we have a booth in the Tiny Wanderer's wine-tasting tent for the Festival this weekend."

"She was supposed to drink it." Dennis said.

"Dennis, shush." Mac glared at him and pointed again, as if punctuating his anger with his index finger.

"Lacey, did you like that wine too? Did you and Dennis partake in wine drinking in the woods?"

"Yes, but please don't tell my Dad."

"Oh honey, he probably already knows." Millie laughed.

"Can you tell me, and this really important, did you open that bottle of wine and pour the glass of wine for Tim that night?" Mac held his breath.

"Yes, I did. I do it all the time when we have events and Dad always has me help out. Are you saying the wine was poisoned?" Her eyes widened. "Dennis, you poisoned our wine?"

"Lacey, you were supposed to drink it. We were supposed to drink that bottle later that night! I told you to keep it here!" Dennis yelled.

"Ben, get him outta here." Mac said.

Ben grabbed Dennis and took him out of the yard.

"Lacey, Dennis wanted you to drink a very dangerous love potion. Instead Tim wound up drinking it and that is why he acted the way he did. All of the events of the past week must have seemed strange. The love potion ultimately killed Tim." Millie explained. "I don't think Dennis understood what he was messing with. Clearly, Dennis is in love with you and wanted you for himself. His plan just backfired and his brother wound up dead."

"Unbelievable." Lacey closed her eyes and rubbed her temples with both hands.

"It's okay. Dennis will be put on trial, but nothing bad will happen to him." Mac said.

Millie rubbed her back. "Lacey, it is very important that you keep these things to yourself. We don't want people thinking that your former friend was a sorcerer. I am sure this is a whole lot for you. Just know that I will be here to protect you and you have nothing to fear from the magical world. Dennis just recently discovered he was a magic user."

"I won't say anything. Besides, I think my aunt is a curandero in Mexico."

"Well, then there you go! This shouldn't be all that shocking to you!" Millie laughed.

"Thanks for all your help." Lacey hugged Millie tight.

CHAPTER TWENTY-FOUR

Mac and Millie stood in front of the Tiny Wanderer's wine tasting tent. There were a few puffy clouds in the sky and the temperature was around fifty-five degrees. A beautiful day, a perfect day. The Festival of the Vine was in full-swing. Food vendors set up. Horse carriages providing transportation across the brick paced street made quite the contrast from the dark and chilly evening the dynamic duo experienced last night.

Mac nodded and raised his glass to Lacey, who poured his glass of Cabernet Sauvignon. She smiled.

Millie raised her glass too.

"You don't think this is spiked with some crazy love potion, do you?" Mac looked at the glass.

"I don't even care at this point. I just need a drink. All the drinks."

"I love it when you say that. You know, you are pretty funny, Ms. Millie. Shall we take a stroll down our favorite street?" Mac put out his arm for Millie to grab.

"We shall." Millie happily obliged and took his arm.

"What a night. Now, barring any crazy-ass random things happening, this will be the first Geneva event we've been to together that isn't interrupted by murderers."

"Mac don't jinx us. Besides, crazy seems to follow us. I'm sure my family is walking these streets somewhere." Millie looked around facetiously.

"Haha! Your family is fantastic."

"They are actually pretty great. They are a lot, but definitely great."

"I just love this event. It's so nice—and tonight isn't too hot and too cold. I think it's cute that they have the kids do artwork on the streets for this. Let's head down and look at those!" Mac said.

"It is a great event. Lots of wine. Wine makes everything better. Sure, let's head down" She glanced at him. You seem pretty excited."

The pair walked just past the food tent and the courthouse.

"We need to get some food soon." Millie smelled the delectable treats from the food tent.

"We will. Here we are, let's check out the chalk art. Look at this one over here. This one is cool." Mac walked Millie over and pointed his cane at a chalk art message in bright blue and purple.

Mac read aloud the contents of the chalk message, "Here at Festival of the Vine, you would make life divine, if you would be mine now and forever. Millie Paderson, will you marry me?"

Millie's head didn't move from the message. Head down. Staring at the message written in chalk.

Mac dropped his cane, winced, and knelt down, opening a small box containing a diamond ring with blue sapphires in the band.

She kept staring at the message.

Mac finally moved and knelt on the message. Ring out. Eyes connecting to hers.

"Yes, I will!" Millie screamed.

The book that started it all!

Add 'Catch a killer' to your Christmas to-do list!

In this delightful cozy mystery set in downtown Geneva, Illinois, our sarcastic and savvy sleuths will seek justice for the untimely death of the owner of the beloved and charming retail mansion: The Tiny Wanderer.

"Millie has requested that I formally query you for your opinion of this crazy night in Autumn in the form of a book review. So please leave a review of "The Festival of the Vine" We thank you very much. Also please my follow my buddy JB to keep in touch with him.

JB Michaels on Facebook!

JB on Amazon!

JB on Twitter!

JB on Instagram!

MAC, NON-WRITER AND RETIRED
CHICAGO COP.

Copyright © 2020 by JB Michaels

All rights reserved.

No part of this book may be reproduced in any form or by any electronic or mechanical means, including information storage and retrieval systems, without written permission from the author, except for the use of brief quotations in a book review.

 Created with Vellum

FIVE CHAPTER EXCERPT OF "THE CASTLE" FROM JB'S SPOOKY SERIES 'CHRONICLES OF THE ORDER'

DATE NIGHT

THE CANDLELIGHT FLICKERED. The soft glow accentuated his finely drawn cheekbones and strong jawline. His blue eyes bore a look of joy in the laughter he shared with his female companion. The brunette with the green eyes and ruby-red lipstick closed her eyes and laughed, nearly spilling the wine from her medieval goblet. Before she stopped giggling and her eyes reopened in recovery of her jovial fit, his brow furrowed. His eyes showed his true condition—a menacing yet brief look, one of lust and of hunger in full and equitable measure. The look vanished. His courtly composure retained.

"Oh, my dear Vincentas, who knew you could be so amusing?"

"Shall I take umbrage with your last statement and just kill you right now?" Vincentas grinned.

Another loud burst of laughter.

The Cabernet Sauvignon didn't have a higher level of spirits than any other wine he usually picked from his cellar. Still, Vincentas poured more into her goblet. His attempts at humor could land, but usually with a casual, rather weak effect. She acted as if he'd performed a comedy routine for years and had earned his own television show.

"That is enough wine for me, Vincentas. What are you trying to do me?" She leaned over the small table, giving him full view of her cleavage.

"I do nothing that one does not allow amicably." He smiled, leaned forward, and kissed both of her cheeks then pulled back to survey her reaction.

She stood up from her chair, took another swig from her goblet, walked to his side of the table, and pulled him off his chair. She grasped his shirt collar with both hands and kissed him like a lioness devoured a fresh kill. Her aggression took Vincentas by surprise.

She wasn't the real monster though.

The candlelight moved violently, then the flames extinguished, and darkness overtook the room.

Vincentas didn't need the light. His hands caressed her where they had touched many other women in his long life. He loved discovering the slight variations of the female physique. The curves, the hips, the muscles both hard and soft, the flesh. His particular favorite: the length of the neck.

She moaned.

The sensual and soft sounds of sexual assurance turned to a panicked scream.

A loud crash filled the dark room. In the struggle to free herself, she kicked over the dinner table.

"No! No! Please! Plea—" Her voice gargled with blood.

The wicks of the candles were once again alight with flame.

Vincentas held his prey in both arms and feasted on his favorite body part. Perhaps his enthusiasm got the best of him. He lifted his head from her neck and spit out a piece of her vocal cords, then dropped her on the stone floor.

He sighed, looked up, and shook his head.

"Much needed. Much needed."

A voice from behind him called, "I take it she wasn't suitable."

"Just another eager gold digger, I am afraid. Take this husk away. I need to work on my compositions anyway."

CHAPTER TWENTY-SIX

ARRESTED DEVELOPMENT

BUD STOOD in his grandfather's home, his mouth agape. The ordeal he thought had ended with sealing the nasty poltergeist into a tree in Chicago's Jackson Park continued on. At least Maeve, an empathic monk of the Order of St. Michael, and Ivy, his newest friend and amateur archaeologist, were with him. Bud's inclination to retreat from humanity in tough times had started to change and reverse with the trials of the last couple days. His android companion, Bert, had malfunctioned and threw himself off the top of the Willis Tower and then rampaged his way into the Art Institute where Bud was forced to behead the fellow.

Bud continued to stare at the mess of his old office. The broken computer monitor screen still sparked. His keyboard was cracked in half. The tree symbol was carved into the wood of his desk.

"We need to find out everything we can about that symbol." Ivy traced the split wood with her fingers.

"It's not the first time we have seen it." The newly rejuvenated Maeve went to stand next to Ivy.

Bud's attention had shifted again to the desecrated pictures and dismantled frames that held pictures of him and his grandfather. His chest heaved repeatedly. Waves of anger, sadness, and then despair struck the heart of the young genius-inventor.

"Bud, you okay?" Maeve turned to see Bud's inconsolable state.

"He is still out there somewhere. He must be. Why would the assailants who penetrated this house target these pictures? They must... Why?" Bud shook his head.

"It might not mean anything, Bud. They trashed the whole house. Perhaps, it would be best to not get too caught up in the pictures," Ivy said.

"Ivy's right. Whoever did this is messing with you, Bud. It doesn't mean they know anything about your grandfather's whereabouts. What is more disturbing is that someone stole some of your precious tech, shut down your teleportation wristband, and of course Bert's head," Maeve said.

"Any rivals at school or in general, Bud? I mean, let's face it, you aren't the most lovable guy on the planet. A disgruntled spouse whose marriage you ruined with your PI investigations?" Ivy pressed.

"Not likely. The tree connects to when Bud and I first met. Brother Mike had tree symbols all over his teacher edition textbook. Brother Mike is doing hard time. Though he could have had an accomplice that we don't know about, I suppose."

"Do we call the cops or what?" Ivy asked.

"No, that is probably not a good idea."

"Bud Hutchins! Hands up! Now!" A deep male voice sounded from the front hall.

"No need to summon the police. Not to worry. I have been through this before." Bud put his hands up.

The police officer removed his right hand off the gun in his holster and brought out the handcuffs. "Keep them up!"

"You've been arrested before?" Ivy asked.

"Yes, he has," Maeve interjected.

"Indeed." Bud felt the cold metal of the cuffs on his wrists, this time without the comfort of teleportation to provide an escape.

CHAPTER TWENTY-SEVEN

RIVALS IN JUSTICE

BUD HAD BEEN in a similar state before—the state of criminal arrest. This time, the surroundings were much different. The quaint, wood-paneled, cozy atmosphere of the Salem police department building contrasted with the square room with white walls, bright fluorescent lighting, and a large mirror adorning the wall of the Chicago police precinct he now sat in. The place smelled of urine. Many suspects apparently lost control of their bladders in the interrogation room. Bud's leather jacket squeaked and sounded as he shifted in his chair.

"Ahh...Hutchins, dat right?" A large man with a

thick mustache entered the room. He embodied the image of stereotypical Chicago sports fan. He examined a flip chart and held a tablet computer underneath the chart.

"Yes, Bud Hutchins is my name. I seek no counsel. No need for it. I know my rights."

"Oh, great. I'm Officer Wendt. Just need to ask ya a few questions. You face some pretty serious charges, the worst of which is aggravated battery and that battery happened ta be inflicted on a police officer."

"Must you talk that way? It is rather distracting to count how many needless words you use before you finally spit out what you mean with your thick Chicago accent." Bud didn't mince words, his mood not conducive to making his life easier.

"It is very clear ta me dat you really don't want ta get outta here, do ya? This will be quick, den." Wendt smoothed his tie over his rather large beer gut and sat across from Bud. He thumbed through a few pages on his flip chart then brought out the tablet and fumbled with the button to wake it from sleep mode.

Bud rolled his eyes.

"Deez damn things are a pain in da ass, ya know?" Wendt smiled. The tablet screen finally brightened up. "Dere we go! All righty, dis you, Buddy?" He slid the tablet over to Bud.

"Slide through da pics. We have plenty. Are these all you?"

The pictures showed Bert's rampage with Bud running after the malfunctioning android on Michigan Avenue, in the lobby of the Chicago Symphony Orchestra, then across the street to the Art Institute.

"Yes, that is..."

A muscular, bald man with a blue FBI jacket busted through the door.

"What in da hell? I am in the middle of an interrogation" Wendt stood up, and his belly hit the side of the table and nearly knocked it over.

"We understand that he caused a lot of problems for you and the department, but we are taking him into federal custody. I'm Special Agent Jordan. Mr. Hutchins, you are coming with me."

"Jesus Christ. What bullshit. He smashed one of our guy's hands. He'll have pins in his hands for months!" Wendt didn't seem to want to let Bud go.

"Wonderful. Officer Wendt proved most annoying if I might say so." Bud stood up to leave the room with Jordan.

"You shouldn't say so. You are in deep shit,

Hutchins. Wendt send over everything you have on this kid, please, asap. I already have some of your people doing that. Just make sure I get everything I need and ask for." Jordan walked over to Bud then cuffed him again.

Bud hoped that Maeve and Ivy were monitoring his situation. He had no idea where the intimidating federal agent would take him.

CHAPTER TWENTY-EIGHT

BUSTED BUD

"THIS ISN'T GOOD." Maeve leaned forward and gripped the steering wheel of Bud's parents' sedan that she and Ivy had borrowed.

Bud was escorted by a scary federal agent into a black SUV outside of the Chicago Police station on 111th and Vincennes. The streetlamp's amber glow didn't provide much light to get a good look at the agent. He was big and black in contrast to Bud's pasty whiteness.

"Shit. That's the FBI. That car looks FBI-ish." Ivy leaned forward as well then pulled her glasses from her face and wiped the lenses. "Definitely FBI.

The federal government is taking him. That complicates matters."

Maeve shifted into drive. "We have to follow them."

"They are most likely going downtown on the Dan Ryan. FBI has an office downtown," Ivy said, still not fully recovered from nearly being killed by Professor Covington-turned-Mr. Hyde. The monster who drank an improperly prepared ancient elixir would haunt her indefinitely.

The black SUV traveled east on 111th St. to the expressway.

"Well, if you are gonna tail someone, might as well be a high-speed one." Maeve turned onto the expressway behind Bud and the black SUV.

"What do you mean tail? Don't you think we should try and bust him out of there before he gets to the FBI headquarters?" Ivy asked.

"You have a point. I mean, I was thinking the same thing. I just didn't know you would be game for this." Maeve smirked, pushed down hard on the accelerator.

Chicago's Dan Ryan expressway was a huge multi-lane expressway that ran south to north toward downtown. The many cars darting between lanes would provide good cover.

"Wait, wait, we should think about this a bit more." Ivy pulled out her phone and examined locations that could be suitable to run the SUV down.

Maeve slowed and stayed two cars behind Bud and the FBI agent.

"What you thinking Ivy?" Maeve looked over.

"Well, if they stay on 94, we will be forced to run them down and bump or block them on an exit ramp. If the FBI guy exits to Lake Shore Drive, then we have plenty of room to push them off the road, and that will most likely be clear of civilians. I mean, it's almost eleven." Ivy kept scrolling through the map on her phone.

"Okay, so we just chill and make our move when we get closer to downtown." Maeve eyed the SUV ahead of them.

BUD LOOKED out the tinted window of the black SUV at the White Sox ballpark, which had changed corporate sponsorship so many times that even he, the genius, couldn't remember its official name. Most people referred to it as Comiskey, even though the miserly owner of Chicago's original baseball team had sold the franchise years ago.

"Hutchins. You are connected to some pretty

incredible and dangerous tech. We have been keeping tabs on you ever since you popped up in London and busted Robbie McGann and provided the murder weapon that matched wounds in bodies at locations in Salem, Louisiana, and Wales. Pretty interesting that you are tied to a weapon that killed so many people in such a small span of time across such great distances. Then we saw surveillance feeds of you vanishing from the Medieval Armor gallery in the Art Institute with the head of a robot in your hand. You seem to be around some pretty impressive things and perhaps even done some incredible things." Agent Jordan didn't seem to want to wait to get to the office downtown to begin.

"I am impressive. Of that I can assure you, Special Agent." Bud grinned.

"It's too bad the CPD wants to charge you with aggravated assault. It's also too bad that your inventions cannot be allowed to exist without endangering others," Agent Jordan said, all the while keeping his eyes on the road.

"I am fully aware that I have certain inalienable rights and don't have to converse with you on such matters." Bud shook his head.

"I could just turn you back over to the CPD, Mr.

Hutchins." Agent Jordan gave Bud a snide look, one Bud was used to giving, not receiving.

"OH, oh. He is going to Lake Shore Drive." Ivy pointed.

"I got it. Okay, so what is the plan?" Maeve merged to the right and kept pace behind the SUV.

"Once we get past the Museum Campus and Soldier Field, try to force him off the road to the left. There is a grassy hill that leads to the lake shore, and there is no beach there. Let's not wind up in the lake."

Signs for Lake Shore Drive North were posted above them, their green with white lettering clear in the ambient light of the big city. The McCormick Place convention complex was on their right and stretched over the road with a walking bridge and extended to another building on their left. They drove parallel to Lake Michigan. Soldier Field and its mighty columns was up ahead, and behind that, the Field Museum.

"Get ready to make your move, Maeve."

"I got this." Maeve gripped the wheel harder. When they merged onto Lake Shore, the traffic had dwindled but not enough to ensure no one else would get hurt. Still, no car was between Bud's SUV and them.

"See that Brontosaurus skeleton on the right next to the Field Museum? That is when you should make your move." Ivy pointed to the paleontological specimen.

AGENT JORDAN DROVE at about fifty miles per hour around the slight right curve beyond the Field Museum.

Silence had filled the car. Bud didn't want to talk. He was too smart to incriminate himself regardless of the various camera feeds that showed him running after Bert all over downtown. Bud pondered the possibility that perhaps he would be better off with the CPD than the federal government, but he knew Jordan wouldn't give him up. It was all too obvious why the government wanted him. A genius like Bud needed to be cultivated, used, but also controlled.

"Oh, Hutchins. I guess I will make a phone call to the CPD."

Bud felt the heat under his seat. The smoke billowed from his feet resting comfortably on the all-weather floormats.

"Agent Jordan, your pathetic, macho posturing should summarily cease. Your government-issued lemon is on fire." Bud coughed from the smoke billowing from the undercarriage.

"What the hell did you do, Hutchins? Shit!" Agent Jordan looked back, then rolled the windows down. The FBI Agent pulled the car to the eastern curbside of Lake Shore Drive and hopped out of the car. Flames danced underneath. The tires melted.

"You will unlock the door, you bumbling buffoon." Bud kept his cool. He coughed though. A lot and wretchedly. It would only be a few seconds until the flames hit the gas tank.

CHAPTER TWENTY-NINE

SAFE BOAT

AGENT JORDAN TOOK off his jacket, wrapped it around his muscly arm and hand, and approached the SUV's door handle. The tongues of orange flames licked at the door. The law enforcement officer pulled the hot handle.

Bud tumbled out of the car.

"Better run, Hutchins!" Agent Jordan grabbed Bud and ran toward the lake and out of traffic on Lake Shore Drive.

Bud craned his neck around to the road. About twenty feet in front of the burning SUV was his beat-up old Grand Am. He smiled.

"How in the hell does a brand new SUV erupt into flames? Jesus Christ." Agent Jordan panted and kept a strong grip on Bud's arm.

"I don't surmise a wise, middle-aged prophet had anything to do with the car's poor build quality." Bud watched the SUV burn.

The flames grew more intense as they met the gas tank. The explosion heated Bud's face. His ears pained from the booming sound.

"Shit. My phone was in the car!" Agent Jordan shook his head.

"Shan't we wait for the emergency responders? Assuredly, they can bring us to FBI headquarters."

"Oh, is that where you think you are going?"

"WELL, setting the car on fire wasn't what I had in mind. I thought you were going to ram them and force them to pull over that way. Or at least get us into a high-speed chase on Lake Shore. Ugh." Ivy couldn't believe it.

"This old beater would never be able to take on that SUV. Using my powers seemed like the better route. Now all Bud has to do is pull away from him and join us in the car."

"That FBI guy looks pretty strong. I don't think

our gangly, cerebral friend has the brawn to get away from him." Ivy looked on as Bud and the FBI agent walked past their car.

Bud looked at Ivy and Maeve and subtly shook his head.

"Well, great. Now what?" Maeve shook her head and bit her bottom lip.

"We can follow him on foot. Just let them get a decent lead, and we will ditch the car," Ivy said.

"Where could they be going? Why don't they just get a cab or wait for the cops to give them a ride?" Maeve watched Bud and Jordan get smaller and smaller in the distance.

"Good point. Could mean they are close to wherever they need to be. Let's head out." Ivy opened the car door and walked to the sidewalk next to Lake Michigan. Grant Park was across the street to her right and the harbor to her left. Sailboats aplenty.

Maeve exited through the passenger side to avoid traffic, and they pursued Bud on foot.

"I TAKE it you have no intention of officially arresting me and allowing me due process. I believe the distinction to rid a man of their inalienable rights is to deem him or her an enemy combatant. To

Gitmo I go, is it?" Bud kept talking to calm his nerves.

"You are a clever young man, Mr. Hutchins. I will give you that. We are almost to our destination. It's just up ahead. The dock is close. Now can you shut the hell up until I ask you to talk?"

"Oh, lovely. I do warn you that I suffer from seasickness at the sight of a boat that I know I will be on. Even on approach, my stomach churns like a hamster beginning its evening exercise in its cage wheel."

"Hutchins. Jesus." Agent Jordan's eyes grew wider, and his grip tightened on Bud's arm.

"Again, with the Jesus reference. Must you be so pedestrian with your cursory words? A good 'holy shit' or 'hell' would suffice."

"I didn't take you for a religious kid, Hutchins. You sure like to defend Jesus."

"No defense, just a mere call for vernacular variety." Bud's stomach turned over as Agent Jordan pulled him out onto the dock and to a medium-sized yacht. It was black. Difficult to see in the low ambient light of the lakefront.

"Here we are." Agent Jordan yanked Bud with more force and climbed the dock stairs. Another FBI

Agent unlocked the gate to enter the deck of the black yacht.

"Jordan," the new agent said.

"Johnson. Meet Bud." Agent Jordan brought Bud in front of him and pushed him up the dock stairs and onto the deck of the yacht.

Bud began to hiccup. The boat already bothered him.

CHAPTER THIRTY

CABIN FEVER

"A BOAT? Are we sure these guys are FBI?" Maeve said.

"The license plate was government issued for sure." Ivy looked at the yacht from the sidewalk next to the dock.

"How do we get him out of there?" Maeve asked.

"As long as they stay put, I have an idea. See that blue and white sailboat next to it on the other side of the dock? Hide in it. Give me the keys to the car."

Maeve handed the keys to Ivy. "Here you go. Where are you going?"

"Back to campus real fast. I need a few things."

"Hurry up. These guys creep me out," Maeve said.

"Really? You are a monk of the Order of St. Michael. You have seen some crazy shit in your life."

"Yes, paranormal I can handle. Dangerous humans give me more cause for worry."

"Whatever. I am off. Be back soon. I promise!" Ivy ran back toward the Grand Am.

Maeve made her way to the blue and white sailboat to do some recon.

BUD LOOKED AROUND, yet again finding himself in captivity. This time there was a porthole in front of him. Cherry-wood finish all around. The room's furnishings held a regal, yet contemporary look with plush green seating and a smell of hard liquor, like cognac. Still, his stomach turned over, and the hiccups increased.

Agent Jordan walked in with a lemon-lime soda can. "Figured this could help settle your stomach there, little guy."

"I don't—drink that." Bud hiccupped.

"Suit yourself. Just don't blow chunks on me or the floor." Agent Jordan picked up a bucket from the floor and put it on the table Bud sat behind. "Now to business, Hutchins. The American government, your country, will be willing to negotiate a pardon for your crimes. Get the CPD to let you go, if you are willing to cooperate."

"What is it...ack... What is it that you want?" Bud asked.

"We want your tech. We are willing to give you all the resources you need to invent, reinvent, and innovate for Uncle Sam."

Bud was right. They wanted his brain. He would have reveled more in his glory of being right once again, but his sickness worsened.

"You do realize, Hutchins, that we are not sailing? What is wrong with you?" Agent Jordan asked.

"It is of no matter. We are still on the water. The answer is no. I will not be under the employ or indentured servitude of the federal government."

"So, you would rather go to jail?! The evidence against you is overwhelming! I will be back in a little bit. Let you think on it." Agent Jordan stood up and slammed the cabin door.

MAEVE CROUCHED behind the mast of the sailboat Ivy had directed her to. She eyed the porthole of the black yacht, its light indicating Bud's location. She hoped.

"Ivy, hurry the hell up." Maeve drove her hands into her armpits, begrudging the cold Lake Michigan breeze.

The young monk of the Order of St. Michael waited and waited. She felt different since Bud had dumped an ancient elixir down her throat to revive her from a damaged, undead state. The more she thought about the last few months since she'd met Bud, the more emotional: the loss of her uncle to a killer hellbent on reviving an evil pagan god, her crazy whirlwind adventures with Bud all over the US and the UK, her subsequent death, undeath, and transformations to a werewolf were all wiped away by a drink that Ivy had concocted.

Sometimes, even with her training in combatting the occult, Maeve had a hard time believing the insanity of her experiences. Still, her resolve to serve the Order had been steeled by the last few months. This is who she was meant to be—a holy warrior against the supernatural forces of evil.

"Hands up!" a gruff voice yelled.

"Okay. Okay!" Maeve quickly raised her hands. A supernatural warrior, not a natural warrior.

The agent grabbed her arm and nearly dragged her out of the sailboat.

"You are one of his friends. We recognized you. Didn't you think we had the entire harbor under surveillance? You kids lack common sense sometimes." The FBI agent pushed Ivy to the stairs of the black boat.

Maeve climbed the stairs. She bit her lip and wanted to wipe the deck with the ignorant, aggressive agent. But she kept her head down, and he pushed toward another set of stairs to the cabin where Bud was held.

"Oh, you blithering idiot, Maeve. Your imprisonment greatly reduces our odds of getting away from these brutish government agents." Bud's eyes were wide open, along with his mouth.

Maeve wanted to jam his big mouth shut.

"Why did I even bother attempting to rescue you again?" Maeve glared at Bud.

The agent pushed down on her shoulders. She sat right next to Bud. They were both summarily detained.

USA TODAY BESTSELLING AUTHOR
JB MICHAELS
THE VIKING
THRONE
THE CURSED SEAS COLLECTION